SIREN
Publishing

Ménage Everlasting

MADE MEN 6:
THE ROOT
OF ALL EVIL

DIXIE LYNN DWYER

Made Men 6: The Root of All Evil

Giada doesn't think she can ever love again, and definitely not men who live dangerous lives. She lost her first and only love to combat. Getting involved with made men wouldn't be smart at all.

In an attempt to avoid the feelings she has for the Coglonie men, she gives in to a small attraction to two very sexy clients who put her on edge and are *definitely* interested in taking her to bed. Little does she know, they're connected to a Cuban gang and potential enemies of the Coglonies. Trying to avoid the dangers of being a woman to made men could actually put her into a worse predicament, after all.

Andreas, Dominick, and Giuseppe Coglonie won't accept Giada's denial any longer. They make her see that their love is real and so powerful it can't be avoided. As she accepts their love, they make more demands she isn't ready to commit to—and it nearly costs her life.

Because they are unaware of an enemy out for revenge against them, abducting the most important person in the Coglonie men's lives will give him the revenge he is looking for.

Genre: Contemporary, Ménage a Trois/Quatre, Romantic Suspense
Length: 65,352 words

MADE MEN 6: THE ROOT OF ALL EVIL

Dixie Lynn Dwyer

Siren Publishing, Inc.
www.SirenPublishing.com

A SIREN PUBLISHING BOOK

MADE MEN 6: THE ROOT OF ALL EVIL
Copyright © 2017 by Dixie Lynn Dwyer

ISBN: 978-1-64010-829-5

First Publication: October 2017

Cover design by Les Byerley
All art and logo copyright © 2017 by Siren Publishing, Inc.

PUBLISHER
Siren Publishing, Inc.
www.SirenPublishing.com

DEDICATION

Dear readers,

Thank you for purchasing this legal copy of *Made Men 6: The Root of All Evil.*

May you enjoy this story about Giada and her journey to love again after facing such loss and heartache. For such a petite woman, she sure is a powerhouse. She stands her ground, fights when pushed to the edge or threatened, and, more importantly, fights for love and for her men.

The fears she has are justified, but she soon realizes that the power of her attraction to Andreas, Giuseppe, and Dominick is much stronger and more valuable than anything they have worked for and achieved in life.

They say that money is the root of all evil. Perhaps that's true, when it becomes your sole purpose for living and breathing instead of the simple things like love, laughter, companionship, empathy, and simply belonging.

Enjoy Giada's story.

Happy reading.

Hugs,
Dixie

ABOUT THE AUTHOR

People seem to be more interested in my name than where I get my ideas for my stories from. So I might as well share the story behind my name with all my readers.

My momma was born and raised in New Orleans. At the age of twenty, she met and fell in love with an Irishman named Patrick Riley Dwyer. Needless to say, the family was a bit taken aback by this as they hoped she would marry a family friend. It was a modern day arranged marriage kind of thing and my momma downright refused.

Being that my momma's families were descendants of the original English speaking Southerners, they wanted the family blood line to stay pure. They were wealthy and my father's family was poor.

Despite attempts by my grandpapa to make Patrick leave and destroy the love between them, my parents married. They recently celebrated their sixtieth wedding anniversary.

I am one of six children born to Patrick and Lynn Dwyer. I am a combination of both Irish and a true Southern belle. With a name like Dixie Lynn Dwyer it's no wonder why people are curious about my name.

Just as my parents had a love story of their own, I grew up intrigued by the lifestyles of others. My imagination as well as my need to stray from the straight and narrow made me into the woman I am today.

Enjoy *The Root of All Evil* and allow your imagination to soar freely.

For all titles by Dixie Lynn Dwyer, please visit
www.bookstrand.com/dixie-lynn-dwyer

MADE MEN 6: THE ROOT OF ALL EVIL

DIXIE LYNN DWYER
Copyright © 2017

Prologue

Giada was fuming mad and a little scared walking into the back room of Govan's bar. It was a dive and a place she wouldn't get caught dead in. Unfortunately for her, Uncle Les was in trouble—again.

She came prepared, or she hoped she was prepared, with her can of mace and loose clothing so she could defend herself if she needed to use her martial arts moves. She'd gotten a call from some guy who said her uncle got beaten up and been left in the back alley of their place. He asked they didn't call the cops but instead call her. She didn't know why. Giada hadn't spoken with Uncle Les since the Coglonie men took over protection for her. That was months ago. She had been so angry that he'd insulted Rayanna and even the Coglonie men. If it weren't for Andreas, Giada would be dead.

"You Giada?" some big guy asked her as he looked her over.

"Yup."

"We put him in the back hallway. He's all frigged up. Not sure if you want to take him to the hospital," the guy said to her.

For a big bouncer-type guy with a beard and a rugged air about him, he seemed kind. "I suppose he won't want to go. God knows what he got himself into."

When she rounded the corner and saw Uncle Les leaning against the wall all battered, nose bleeding, eye swelled out badly, she cringed. She shouldn't be here. The man only showed up in her life when he needed money, wanted to pretend he cared and be part of her life, and when he was down and out. They weren't close—never had been—so why was she even here?

"Who did you piss off this time?" she asked him.

"I'm sorry, Giada. There wasn't anyone else to call."

"I don't need any trouble, Uncle Les. I don't, not after the past six months I've had."

She went to help him up, and he struggled. "It's not that bad. They could have killed me."

She looked at the guy who helped him inside. "Thanks for the help. Sorry if he caused any trouble."

"No problem, honey. He isn't welcome back, but you, you can stop by anytime." He winked.

She gave a slight smile, well, not really. It was more out of being polite than anything to avoid any more trouble. She helped her uncle outside and then leaned him up against the wall.

"So what's the deal?"

"No deal. It's good. I just need a little help."

"Money?"

"Just to get me by. I'm going to get a job. It's coming through this week, a good one, too."

"I don't want to hear it, Uncle Les. In fact, I thought I told you our relationship was over."

He looked at her. "Because of those no-good thugs hounding you? You're a good woman, a beautiful young woman who deserves a man who can take care of you and love you, not use you. I did what I did, said those things to those gangsters for your own good. Be mad at me all you like. I saved you from being used goods."

She rolled her eyes. "You didn't save me from anything."

"They're not around anymore, right?"

"No. The danger is over."

He grabbed onto her as she hailed a cab. "Stay clear of them, Giada. Listen to me. I'm taking care of everything. I'm making things up to you. I'm getting things better."

"What are you talking about? It's the middle of the night, in the middle of the week, and I'm dragged out of bed to come get you from a shit bar all beaten up, and you're talking to me about making things right? I don't need or want anything from you, Uncle Les. What I want is for you to straighten yourself out, get a job, and leave me be. I'm fine taking care of myself."

"You aren't fine if those gangsters are still sniffing around you. You need a man who can protect you from thugs like those guys, someone who respects your profession and beauty and will protect you from the harm men like the Coglonies can cause you." He was rambling.

"What are you even talking about?"

"Nothing. You'll see. Just stay clear of those men. There are better men out there for you. You'll see."

"My life is not your concern. I think you need to focus more on your life."

They got into the cab, and she told the driver where to take him. She would make the trip to Queens, drop him off, and head back to Manhattan.

"You going out Friday night?" he asked her.

"Why?"

"Just asking. You should stay clear of Club X. That's where those guys hang out, right?"

"Who?"

"You know who. Coglonic."

"They own that club and others, too."

"They're not good for you."

"Stop it," she warned, and he was silent.

"I'm sorry I keep failing you as an uncle and as your family. I know the two of us is all we got left. I'm going to make things right."

"There's nothing to make right. Just stay out of trouble. You keep messing with the wrong guys, and you'll end up dead."

She leaned back, waiting for the cab to get to her uncle's small house. He got out, and she handed him some money. "Try not to spend it foolishly."

He nodded. "I'll pay you back. I'll make it so you won't need to work another day in your life."

He then stumbled to his door. She told the cab driver to wait a moment. She wanted to be sure her uncle got inside okay. Once he was inside, the cab driver headed back to Manhattan, an expensive cab fare in the middle of the night on a Tuesday. She glanced at her watch. She had three hours until she needed to get up for work. What the hell kind of trouble had he gotten into, and why had he asked her to come get him? She leaned back and covered her mouth as she yawned. Never again. She wasn't going to do this again.

* * * *

Uncle Les looked out the window and watched Giada leave. He was shaking he was so scared. He hadn't wanted to call her, but they had given him no choice. He was in over his head. He had to promise them something. He knew that the Coglonie men wanted his niece in their beds. She meant something to them, but they were no good for her. They were made men, thugs who did violent shit, even killed people. These men, the ones who approached him, wanted to destroy the Coglonies and the Fiorre family. Their boss had a lot of money and power and was a good-looking older guy. He would make a better husband for Giada, and he wouldn't want to share her with his friends or anyone else. That wasn't even normal.

He ran his fingers through his hair. His body ached, and his nose and eye throbbed. He had no idea they had been following him and had seen Giada, watched her for the last couple of months. These men had connections, and they could just take her right now if they wanted to, but that wasn't what they were after. They wanted to destroy the two families, specifically Dominick and Giuseppe Coglonie. They could do that. Plus, he could make some money and work for them, too, and Giada would be set for life, would have a man who would take care of her, provide for her, and protect her.

She was a tiny thing, feminine and sweet, but also successful, smart, and sexy. The man was instantly interested in Giada and went from wanting to take her to hurt the Coglonies to wanting her for himself. Les would make things right. He would get her out of trouble and going down the wrong path with the Coglonies and have her married into a powerful, wealthy family.

So what they weren't from New York and wouldn't be living here. He would have enough money to go see her, and she could even send for him and pay for it, as well. It would work out for both of them. Now he just had to sit and wait for the orders to come in, not go looking for trouble like he had tonight. That could have destroyed the plan and his deal with the man in charge. He needed to be smart. He wouldn't let Giada make the wrong decisions. He was the only family she had left. It was his job to protect her.

* * * *

Giada Slane walked back into her office in the executive wing of the bank's corporate headquarters. It was a busy morning, and the weekend was finally in sight. She had a lunch meeting with two potential new clients for the firm, along with her boss, Monterro Spain. She handed over some folders to her assistant, Julia.

"That meeting lasted kind of long. I thought he just needed a few minutes," Julia said to Giada.

"Me, too, but I guess Monterro is enthusiastic about these new clients we're meeting today for lunch."

"Who are they anyway?" Julia asked.

"I don't even know. Just that they're international investors or something. He wants to impress them and of course made reservations at Rinaldi's uptown."

Julia's eyes widened, and she smiled. "Yummy. You are so lucky. I hear that place is amazing."

"I've only been there one time before, and personally, I wouldn't drop that kind of money on lunch, and dinner is a mortgage payment for most people."

"You don't need to tell me. My idea of fancy and splurging is at Celia's down on Hendrickson Avenue. I'd pay a meal's price for their mocha martini."

Giada chuckled. "I would, too. They are amazing. In fact, I'm supposed to meet some friends there on Friday night. If you want to join us, you should come along."

"Aw, man, I can't. I'm babysitting for my sister and her husband. They haven't been out alone since the baby was born nine months ago. I promised."

"Aw, that's so sweet of you. I love babies. You're a good sister." Giada's cell phone buzzed with a message. She glanced down, looked at the text, and smiled. "It's a day away, and the ladies are already texting about Friday night." She chuckled.

"Don't rub it in. I'll be elbows-deep in dirty diapers, bottles, and Einstein videos when you'll be drinking my martini," Julia said.

Giada gave her a sympathetic smile. "Next time. Right now you're being an angel."

Julia smiled. "Thanks, Giada."

Giada walked into her office and sat down at her desk. She needed to hit the ladies' room, reapply her lip gloss, and make sure she looked good for this meeting. She had no idea who these men were, but by her boss's insistence on perfection and impressing them, they were loaded. Monterro had even mentioned that bonus coming her way and the raise in salary. She'd earned it, despite missing work for a few weeks. That had been two months ago, after the concussion.

She ran her hand along the back of her head. Thank God she no longer had the headaches or the ringing in her ears. She texted Fina, Alessa, Alda, and Donata back in the group chat.

I can't wait either. I have a client meeting so take me off group text. See you tomorrow night at Celia's at six.

Fina texted back. *We're going to hit a few places after so dress to kill and look superhot so we can get into the clubs. Wear your dancing shoes, Giada.*

Giada exhaled. She really needed this night out. It would be the first in weeks, and finally the idea of loud music, crowds, and drinking didn't make her head ache and her stomach hurt. Maybe things were finally getting back to normal again?

That thought made her look back at her phone and the text just last week from Andreas Coglonie. He had been checking in on her, and she had blown him off just like she had been since Rayanna had been found safe and sound and Puento was no longer a problem. More than two months had passed. She thought about Rayanna and seeing her in a couple of weeks when she visited New York. Hopefully she would look and feel a lot better than she had months ago.

Giada swallowed hard. Seeing what Rayanna had gone through and knowing about the dangers of being involved with made men were the perfect remedy to stop her from getting involved with Dominick, Giuseppe, and Andreas. She feared them for so many reasons, despite being attracted to them. It would never work. They were so much older and more experienced. Plus, they were huge, filled with muscles, and she was petite. Taking martial arts classes and kickboxing had built her confidence and was how she'd met Jimmy. He was an instructor when he wasn't called to active duty.

She exhaled, the ache in her heart still pretty tender after losing him two years ago. Then she thought about Andreas again and about the fact that he was Special Forces, just like Jimmy had been. Andreas had that look in his eyes. Everyone was guilty, up to something, and he was distrustful to boot. He was very attractive, had all those muscles, and wore those suits that made him look more like a secret agent than a made man. Some of his employees worked out at the same dojo she did. She'd heard them talk about him as though he was a god—how many medals he had for being a war hero, how quick and capable he was, and, mostly what stood out to her, how they feared him, saying he wasn't a man to piss off and was a man you wanted by your side in a dangerous situation.

She swallowed hard. At Jimmy's funeral she'd met several of his friends from his troop who had survived. They'd said similar things, and she felt proud to have known him, but after everyone left and went about their lives, she had difficulty moving on with her life without him and had wondered why other soldiers lived and why her soldier had died.

Her eyes welled up with tears, and she pushed thoughts of Jimmy away. She'd trusted him with her body, with being loving and caring with her. Soldiers were special people, but she was different now after losing him. Danger was something she wanted nothing to do with. Made men were dangerous.

The Coglonie men had reputations as powerful, wealthy made men who ran various businesses and were involved with criminal activity. They owned several clubs, bars, and lounges—though she only knew Club X—and supposedly organized meetings for negotiations between bosses in the organized-crime syndicate. Danger, danger, and more danger.

It had been enough nearly being abducted and then nearly killed in her hospital room, all because some psycho was after Rayanna and they were good friends. She still couldn't get over that incident. Nor could she get over how unaffected Andreas was, shooting that man, comforting her, and then walking away. These men were killers, criminals desensitized to violence, which was obvious by their ways of life. She hated violence.

She'd lost her one true love to war, and it had broken her heart. Even knowing that Andreas was Special Forces just like Jimmy shouldn't make her think they were the same or that he was a replacement. There were no replacements. That hit too close to home. It made her think of Jimmy and what they could have had. She couldn't go through that type of heartache again—the worrying, the fears of something bad happening to someone she cared about. Times that by three and Giada would go insane. She needed to focus on her profession and staying single, or at least staying away from made men.

Plus Uncle Les. She really needed to stay clear of him, too. He was always getting into trouble and calling her to help. The other night had been so strange, and when she'd left the cab, she'd felt as if someone was watching her. She'd even had that feeling at the bar, too, as they waited for the cab. It was probably because it was nearly three o'clock in the morning, but it still bothered her.

She took a deep breath and exhaled. The time they shared together with them acting as her bodyguards had caused a lot of problems. Uncle Les was more involved in her life than ever before, and he seemed awfully interested in her profession, too. She didn't trust him, but she kind of used his hatred for the Coglonie men as a means to keep them away from her.

It confirmed the dangers their professions and their family business surrounded them in, and she wasn't interested or willing to go through such fear and pain again. She'd declined offers of dates since Jimmy passed, and even by friends and other guys in the military. Lots of men flirted with her at the gym and asked her out. Losing Jimmy was enough to have gone through. She'd wanted to die. She didn't think she could go on living, but thanks to her friends' support and what Jimmy stood for being a Special Forces soldier and dying in combat, she knew she needed to be strong and make him proud of her. She continued the martial arts classes and even instructed young girls so they, too, would learn self-defense and self-confidence. In fact, she really needed to be sure she didn't drink too much or hang out too late tomorrow night. The first martial arts class she had to teach was at 9 a.m.

She logged off the computer and cleaned up her desk, being sure it was tidy and neat, the way she liked it, before she ran to the ladies' room. She had fifteen minutes, and then it was time to lay on the charm and snag some new big-shot clients. She hoped it was a success.

Chapter 1

"There's money to be made. We know that, but it's dirty business," Sunny said to Mateus and Major.

"No one is saying it isn't, but you just said it. There's money to made. With these new connections Adelina has, and that you and Vinny have been making your way into, there's more to be made. We can tap into a market that isn't saturated," Mateus replied.

Sunny looked at Vinny.

"It will be profitable, but the risks are higher. You're talking getting in on the imported merchandise before other organizations that started this can even get it into the US," Vinny said to them.

Major nodded. "Exactly. It's called business and survival of the fittest. You guys have your in, and we have the manpower to give security and ensure that everything is done with protection and success through Bloodline Securities."

"You know this is going to probably piss off Calvarro Torres," Sunny said to them.

"Fuck him. Calvarro shouldn't have been so quick to not lend a hand in the search for Rayanna," Mateus stated firmly.

"Yeah, or jumped on the bandwagon with the rest of the assholes like Miami Cortez, Bay Bloods gang, Bronnos, and Lupez to screw over Dmitri. That wasn't a wise fucking move, nor will we or Dmitri forget what those fuckheads failed to do. It put them on the list of people to watch out for. Believe me, Dmitri, as well us, all of us, should keep all those dicks on our radar," Major said to them.

"I'm all for expanding to other areas to make a profit, and you're right—this market is not tapped. The Cubans don't have the available resources like we have. Plus, with our connections and established routes, we can be smuggling in other things for profit," Sunny said to them.

Mateus smirked. "Now you're thinking like a boss. We can handle this no problem. We need to meet with some people to discuss the arrangements and the cuts. We'll have Dominick Coglonie set it up at Club X for next week."

"Dominick and Giuseppe really deserve a nice piece of this action, too. They also had the connections, and it will be important that we all work together on this and create a monopoly just in case some dicks want to protest our power of operations," Major added.

"Agreed. I'll talk to him about it and their share in this when I set up the meeting," Mateus said.

"Great. So how is Rayanna doing? Adelina spoke to her last week but really quick. She said Rayanna is working?" Sunny asked.

"Giving Dmitri a headache I'm sure. It's all online, and she's been keeping in contact with her clients here in New York. I think her plan is to work a few private jobs," Mateus told him.

"That could be a security nightmare. She needs around-the-clock protection," Vinny said.

"Exactly, which is why Dmitri will more than likely put a stop to it. It's just too dangerous right now. Dmitri is trying to handle anyone who was willing to take him out or cause his demise when he was searching for Rayanna. He's going after them all and with a vengeance," Major said to them.

"I wouldn't want that man on my bad side or working against me. Not for nothing, but that's one badass fucking Russian, the whole group of them," Vinny said.

"Indeed, but hey, you got yourselves one badass, resourceful woman. She needs protection nonstop, too," Mateus stated.

"Believe me, we know that," Sunny said and looked at Vinny.

"We need to head out. We'll make the arrangements and get things in order for this. You can tell us when you confirm that meeting, and we'll be there," Vinny told them.

They shook hands and then headed out. Sunny was feeling a little uneasy. Maybe because he was just learning to trust and expand business with Mateus and Major Fiorre and their cousins and now they were branching out together. The Costanza family was going through some changes all around, but Sunny's and Vinnie's top priority was keeping Adelina's secret and slowly expanding the empire of security around her. She wasn't liking it one bit.

* * * *

Alajandro Frane couldn't take his eyes off the lovely young woman in front of him, nor could his partner, Toro Miguel. She was gorgeous, from her stunning blue eyes to her long black hair that reached her mid-back. She had a soft smile, full lips, full breasts, and a tiny waist and toned thighs, and, he noticed as she arrived, a nice round ass—petite, feminine, and a completely unexpected bonus to this potential business arrangement. Monterro had been right when he said the woman they would be dealing with was exceptional.

Her boss, Monterro Spain, was a good businessman. The services they provided were exactly what they were looking for to hide their money and use the accounts to transfer and deposit funds on a regular basis. After years of proving themselves in the importing and exporting business and cigar industry, they were powerful, successful men, and they had people working for them so they could enjoy the fruits of their labor. He eyed over Giada Slane's lips and neck. The woman was gorgeous.

"So our businesses require confidentiality with clients and funds transferred and withdrawn. We don't want that accessible through anyone working at your company by typing in some password or something," Toro stated firmly.

"Of course, Mister Miguel. That's not how we operate. We have a substantial client list of businessmen like yourselves who want the security of a bank but the privacy of a personal safe. Only you will be aware of the deposits and withdrawals in the account. However, since this is a business, and a means of providing additional protection and security from fraud, theft, and errors, we collect a ten to fifteen percent fee on the total amount in the account annually," Monterro Spain told them.

"And if we want several accounts, that is the price for your security and maintenance would be ten to fifteen percent on *each* account?" Toro asked.

Monterro nodded. "Usually our clients have two to three accounts and no more, so the fee is standard. The accounts are under a million each. In fact you won't find another bank and finance firm that offers a better rate." Monterro Spain looked nervous.

"Seems pricy to me, Alajandro," Toro said and looked from Monterro to Giada.

"I'm certain we can come up with an agreement that you both feel comfortable with. Tell me, how many accounts are you planning to open up with us if you were to choose Saks and Cain?" Giada asked.

Alajandro stared at her, trying to decide what he liked more about the woman—her eyes, her abundant locks, or that sexy, petite figure? He held firm. "With a fee like that, does it matter?"

"Well, I believe it does. As Monterro mentioned, most of our clients open one to three accounts. If you were planning on additional accounts, perhaps transferring from another bank and keeping most of your business and personal accounts with us here at Saks and Cain, then I'm certain we could come up with a more reasonable percentage than ten to fifteen percent," Giada told him.

Her boss smiled and added, of course, that Giada was right. Then he went on about how secure the corporation was, about how every person had a background check on them, and about he could decide among several employees who had the responsibility of overseeing the totals in each account and then applying the fee. It was at their discretion.

Alajandro stared at Giada and then took a sip of his glass of wine. "Are you on that list, Miss Slane? Because it seems to me you would be trustworthy."

Her eyes widened. "That really isn't my job,"

She replied in a soft tone that was sexy, but he was certain she didn't mean it to be.

"She can handle that if you feel more comfortable. She is quite trustworthy and can make herself accessible with whatever procedures you find necessary to allow her to monitor the accounts. Our employees get a thorough background check, fingerprinting, and approval through government intelligence, as well."

"I'm sure we can come up with ways to make you confident that she's right for the job and will give that personal touch it sounds like you're looking for. After all, those fees are once a year, and she can look everything up in your presence so you confirm the numbers are to the penny," her boss told them.

"Okay, and would it be all right if our own set of security does a background check, fingerprinting, et cetera?" Toro asked.

Alajandro didn't look at him, nor did he smirk. It seemed he liked Miss Slane, as well.

"Giada?" Monterro looked at her, and she swallowed hard.

"It's out of the ordinary, but I suppose if it makes you feel better. How many accounts are you thinking, and approximately how much money if you had to guess a range?" she asked.

"Ten accounts, each with anywhere from five hundred thousand to over five million," he said very calmly.

Her eyes widened, and then she blinked.

Monterro cleared his throat and then gulped. "We'll have to get approval to minimize the fee."

"I'm certain we can get that approval and come up with something comfortable for Mister Frane and Mister Miguel. I mean, seriously, with both of you putting your trust in Saks and Cain for your banking and security needs, I will negotiate terms on your behalf. Our boss is a reasonable man and surely will be more than willing to lower that percentage. In all honesty, he would be out of his mind."

Alajandro gave her a nod. "We look forward to discussing the terms and coming up with a number. Perhaps we could meet again for dinner this time?" he asked but only looked at Giada.

"She would be happy to. We'll talk to our top officials and come up with something reasonable," her boss said.

She looked a little annoyed at her boss, and he wondered why. It seemed that she wasn't just seeing dollar signs as he was. She was impressed and trying to get the best price for them and not be greedy. It was sweet and endearing. The woman was precious.

Chapter 2

Celia's was crowded. Giada and her friends Fina, Alessa, Alda, and Donata went to the bar and ordered their mocha martinis.

"Damn it's crowded. I can't believe how packed it is," Fina said as they had to squeeze their way next to the bar.

"This sucks," Donata stated.

"Sure does," Alda said.

Giada felt the hands on her hips and a man press closer. She turned to look, ready to tell the guy to take a hike, but her eyes locked onto one very attractive older man with a tan complexion and a look of prestige about him. His eyes were dark blue, his hair was black, and he wore a designer dress shirt with a suit jacket and smelled good, really good. He stared down into her eyes.

"So sorry. It's very crowded in here. Can I squeeze in to grab a drink?" he asked, his Hispanic accent thick and deep.

She looked at her friends, who widened their eyes and were totally checking the man out. Fina gave her a nudge, a push to flirt with the good-looking older guy. She shook her head. Giada heard him order a Crown Royal.

"Are you ladies enjoying yourselves?" he asked and eyed over their drinks.

"Not really. It's crowded," Fina said, and they all agreed.

He squeezed his way back next to Giada and stared at her a moment as if he were memorizing her face, her eyes, and her lips. "Well, have a good time. Be careful." He winked at her.

"You are out of your mind. He was fucking hot, and that accent. Jesus, I think my panties are wet, and he wasn't even directing all that sexiness toward me," Donata stated.

Her friends laughed, but Giada felt her cheeks warm. "I don't date. You know that."

"Who said anything about dating? Why not an incredible night of sex with someone like him? My God, he's a fantasy guy, and you just blew him off," Alessa added, looking past Giada as if trying to check out the guy's ass or watch him through the crowd.

He was gorgeous and sexy, but she wasn't interested in dating anyone, never mind having sex just to do it. Two years was a long dry spell but for a good reason. Sex wasn't something to take lightly. Her friends talked a good game, but none of them were sluts. They wouldn't just sleep with anyone they'd just met either.

"She's crazy and lost her mind. It finally happened," Alda said and downed the rest of her mocha martini.

Giada looked around them. The sexy guy was nowhere to be seen. She'd lost her chance, another opportunity, but then again, she didn't want that. She just wasn't interested.

Donata and Fina got bumped. "This sucks," Fina said in annoyance, wiping the bit of martini from her chin that spilled when she was taking a sip and got bumped into.

Giada and her friends decided to head a few blocks over to Merchants, an upscale lounge and bar that had a great dance floor and lots of memorabilia around the room. It was crowded, but the setup was different. There were little enclaves and separate areas to stand or even sit. Alda and Donata hurried ahead, spotting some guys leaving a setup of high stools and tables with thick leather-seated stools. There was just enough room for all of them. Just as Giada squeezed by a group of guys asking her if they could buy her a drink, someone placed a hand on her hip. She grabbed it and turned, ready to remove it, when her eyes locked onto Royce, one of the Coglonies' security guys. She had gotten to know him, Train, Logic, and Brew in the couple of weeks she'd needed security while Puento was being hunted down.

"Hi, Royce. How are you?" She leaned up on tiptoes to kiss his cheek. She ignored the guys behind her and saw how Royce practically snarled at them and moved Giada along. He held her close and then guided her to the right and away from the guys now checking her out.

"I'm good. How are you feeling?" He ran his hand along the back of her head.

She smiled. "All better. No more headaches or ringing in my ears. What are you doing here? Night off?"

"Unfortunately, no. I'm with Logic. We're entertaining some business associates of the bosses. You know, showing the hot places to hang out and pick up gorgeous chicks." He winked.

She chuckled.

"Hey, who's your friend, Giada?" Donata asked, coming up behind her.

Royce checked her out and winked.

"This is Royce."

"Well, come on over and join us, Royce," Donata said.

"He isn't alone. He's here on business with some friends."

"Then grab them and have them come over, too. We don't bite," Donata stated and winked.

Royce chuckled and looked at Giada. "We don't have to if you're uncomfortable with it."

"Why would I be uncomfortable?"

He stared at her. "The bosses. The fact I work for them."

"I'm not getting your concern, Royce. We know one another. You're here with friends, and so am I, and we're hanging out having drinks. What does it have to do with your bosses?"

"I just want you to know that I'm not hitting on you. I wouldn't mess with the bosses and what they want."

She squinted at him. Just then Logic and four businessmen, all very good-looking, approached. Royce introduced her as Logic kissed her cheek hello.

"Come on over. I'll introduce you to my friends," she said, and as she walked, she heard the guys ask about her, and then Royce and Logic said she was taken.

Giada couldn't believe the mixed emotions she felt as the night continued. Her friends were having a ball flirting with the guys, and she was still trying to get over Royce's and Logic's comments about her being taken. It made her uneasy, and she wondered what the hell that comment was about. Maybe Royce and Logic just didn't want the men hitting on her and they were protecting her? A few times Royce and Logic looked at their phones, and one time Logic took a picture of her and her friends, who posed.

When she walked over to the bar to grab another drink, some guys started flirting, and one of them was very handsome. She started talking to him until Royce came up behind her, wrapped an arm around her waist, and pulled her away. She felt guilty for some strange reason, and instead of confronting them, she kept quiet and wound up staying put by the table.

The guys who were business friends Royce and Logic had to entertain were actually very nice and pretty funny, but Giada felt out of sorts. So when she glanced at her watch and saw it was after 1 a.m., she said she needed to head out because she was teaching a class in the morning. Royce told her to wait up a minute and started a whole other conversation with her, making her gut clench and think that he was stalling or trying to get her to stay a little longer. Then she saw Royce nod and smile at someone behind her. When she turned around, she hadn't expected to see Train, one of the Coglonies' guards, show up saying he was giving her a ride home.

"What are you talking about? I don't need a ride home," she said to Train and Royce.

"You got one, sweetheart. Are you ready?" Train asked.

He was kind of scary. He had big, wide shoulders; scruff along his cheeks and chin; tattoos that peeked out from the collar of his shirt; and an expression that warned her to do as he said. He was just as intimidating as the three men he worked for. She thought about Dominick, Giuseppe, and Andreas. Her jaw dropped.

"You were texting them, weren't you? They called you, Train, to come here and to give me a ride home, didn't they?" she asked, raising her voice and putting her hands on her hips.

All three men looked down at her.

"They just want to make sure you get home safely," Train said to her and stared down at her with an expression like "So what? Just listen and do what they say."

She growled low, shook her head, and turned around to say good night to her friends. They were immersed in conversation and laughter with the businessmen, not even noticing what was going on with her. Thank God, because she would never hear the end of this.

"Hey, I'm heading out. I have a class in the morning. You ladies be sure to grab the taxi together," she said to them.

They carried on, complaining about her leaving and saying to her how so many guys were checking Giada out that she didn't need to go home alone. She cringed just imagining the report the Coglonie guards would give their bosses.

"Behave," she warned them, and they laughed. She got kisses and hugs good night, including from Logic and Royce, and then Train guided her out of the bar.

She was certain that he'd noticed the men checking her out, smiling and even asking where she was going, but one stern look from Train and the guys raised their hands up and turned away. When she got outside she saw the bouncers, and by the sidewalk was a Range Rover, running, with black-tinted windows.

"I really don't need a ride home. I'm perfectly capable of getting a cab, taking the subway or bus."

He shook his head. "Why do that when you have Brew and me?" he asked, and then she realized Brew was driving. Another guard of the Coglonie men. She exhaled in annoyance as he opened the side door of the Range Rover and she got inside.

"Hey, Giada. How are you, honey?" Brew asked and winked.

"Hi, Brew. Sorry your bosses dragged you out for no reason. I hope you weren't in the middle of something."

Train got into the front seat.

"No, just cruising and getting ready to end shifts. How was the bar?"

"Crowded," Giada said.

"Boring. Too many assholes to keep count," Train said to him as Brew pulled into traffic and headed toward her apartment building.

She lived in a decent place on the east side of Manhattan. She had security and an apartment too big for one person but more than enough room to entertain. She made good money, had worked really hard for it, and had gotten out of Queens as quickly as she could. Uncle Les was still there. She hadn't heard from him, so hopefully that meant he was staying out of trouble.

She saw Train texting on his cell phone. "You should tell them thank you for the ride but please don't make a habit of it. I take care of myself."

Train looked over his shoulder at her. "They care, Giada. They worry about you after the attempted abduction and then that dick breaking in and trying to kill you."

She felt bad. She knew that situation had affected Andreas a lot. He hadn't let go of her for quite some time after that, and she even fell asleep in his arms from the painkillers. She sighed. "I suppose so, but none of it had anything to do with me, and that danger is over. I can take care of myself. If I couldn't, then they would have gotten me into the van."

"Maybe," Brew said.

Train looked upset. They were nice guys, tough men, and she'd rather have them as friends than enemies, so she should be nice.

"There are a lot of asshole guys out there. You need to be careful. I saw the way men were looking at you and trying to make moves. You need protection," Train stated, sounding angry.

"Well, I appreciate the ride. I guess it's better than dealing with the people on the subways this time of night or getting a cab and paying a lot."

"You're welcome." Train winked.

When they got to her apartment building, they walked her inside and up to her door. She thanked them again and asked them to tell their bosses thanks but that she didn't need this becoming a habit. They nodded and went on their way.

When she got into the apartment, that lonely feeling hit her instantly. She could recall when she first moved in here a couple of years ago how independent she'd felt, how proud to afford this place and live upscale in New York City. Then there were the two weeks Andreas, Giuseppe, Dominick, and their guards had hung around the place taking care of her and watching over her. She swore when that call came in that Rayanna was alive and there was no more danger that the Coglonie men seemed disappointed. She felt it, too, but denied it. There was no way she could be with men like them. She'd been over it a bunch of times. Despite their professions, their ages, and their experiences, it was their sizes that did her in. They could crush her.

She didn't even know if they were violent men, men that demanded control from a girlfriend. She didn't know much, and from what she got a glimpse at while they were here caring for her and listening to them talk about leads and helping Dmitri, they were capable men. They could and would kill to get what they needed or wanted.

She shook her head and went to get undressed. Why was she thinking about this? About them? It would never work. They weren't right for her.

She needed a normal man. A businessman who understood her stresses, who respected her independence and need to make money and work long hours when needed. She didn't need a man telling her what to do or insisting she stop working and just focus on him—on them. No, she needed normal. The Coglonie men weren't normal. Despite the attraction she felt and the feelings of lust and need when they were close, she knew it wouldn't last, and then she would be left all alone once again.

Not happening. Focus on work. Work never caused these types of problems, worries, and troubles. Work kept her going every day.

Chapter 3

"They want to do what?" Giada asked her boss, Monterro Spain.

"Toro Frane and Alajandro Frane would like to go out to dinner to some club, and they have one in mind that is doing a Latin theme Saturday night. Then they will determine if they feel comfortable with you to have their security do the background check, which, of course, will be determined by whether you and I can get the bosses to lower the percentage rate per account."

"This doesn't seem like a typical business meeting to me."

"Giada, they're young, successful businessmen. They do things differently than older men. Instead of stuffy meeting rooms and upscale dinners with classical music playing, they like action, excitement, loud music—some character to their meetings. My understanding is that both men do a lot of business deals while sitting back having drinks in clubs. Alajandro mentioned a regular booth at Cha Cha Cabana."

"That is a pretty upscale nightclub, restaurant, and bar. It's a multilevel place, one of the hardest clubs to get into."

"See, you're young like they are. We older guys can't keep up with that. I wouldn't even know how to get out on a dance floor and cha-cha."

She laughed. "I suppose you're right. I just hope it isn't awkward. I mean dinner, discussing the particulars for this deal, and then dancing? I'm a little unsure."

"Giada, you heard them say the amount of money and the multiple accounts they are interested in opening with this company. You're meeting with Davis in an hour, and I'm certain he'll tell you about the bonus you'll get if you land this deal. It will work out fine. You'll see."

She was nervous as she waited to meet with Davis Saks, one of the main owners of Saks & Cain, to discuss these new clients and what the bank could offer them. It was a lot of money, and she felt that some sort of special deal could be made to accommodate the two businessmen.

Giada had a bit of an uneasy feeling still, but it was minimized an hour and a half later as she sat in the main headquarters in Davis Saks's office and discussed her bonus and the opportunity of a new position as liaison negotiating between Saks & Cain and potential high-end clients.

"Monterro was quite impressed with your negotiating skills at the lunch meeting with Frane and Miguel. He said that you jumped right in securing the potential deal and really made a connection with the clients. That's what we want here at Saks and Cain. If you can pull this off, then the liaison position is yours. There's a list of business people we'd like to snag for business here. It would mean fewer hours at the desk and more negotiating terms, pampering clients, and making them feel that personal touch beyond other banks. I think you would be great, Giada. You have a likable personality, and you're sweet, soft-spoken, professional, and attractive. People like that."

"I appreciate the compliments and the opportunity, sir. You do realize the amount of money these men want to secure in our bank here, don't you?" she asked.

"I do. That's why I'm so thrilled. I'm confident that you can secure this deal."

"It looks promising. Is there more we can offer them, though?"

"What do you mean?"

"I mean a more reasonable arrangement. The fees we place on normal accounts shouldn't apply to accounts this large."

"I've thought about that. There is something we offer very few customers. Monterro came up with it a while back, and perhaps these men may fit the criteria."

"What would that be, Mister Saks?" she asked.

"A private customer label. We have one customer who has been with us for several years now. It was before you came on board and Monterro was working with new potential customers. This individual had a lot of money he needed to secure. Like Mister Frane and Mister Miguel, we negotiated lower rates. However, monitoring the accounts more often was part of the deal. It ensured that they weren't ripped off and we made a great profit from this deal. You see, whatever the largest amount of money was in the account in the year that was what we received ten percent on."

"They agreed to that?"

"Sure did, Giada, because this particular man had five accounts with us, and there was so much money being secured, transferred in and out to overseas accounts, withdrawn, reinvested, et cetera, that if we just went to check and apply the fee when we had the opportunity and permission, the client could make sure his account was much lower, making us lose money. It is a negotiated deal that has worked for the last several years."

"That is pretty impressive, and obviously, the bank has made a nice profit. From what these men are stating in the amount of funds they want secured here at the bank, this is a no-brainer to offer them this private customer deal, is it not?"

He leaned back and stared at her. She felt a little uneasy.

"It is. The thing is I don't want this kind of offer getting out to other people. You must ensure that they don't share this deal with anyone and make it look like it was created just for them."

"That makes sense. It's legit, and nothing illegal is being done here."

"Of course nothing illegal is being done. We wouldn't be in business if there ever was. We simply provide the security and safety for clients' money. Let me go over the details with you and what you can offer them when you go out for dinner and dancing with them."

"You heard about that?" she asked, feeling embarrassed.

"Oh, yes, I did. I think it's a great idea. They are young businessmen and supposedly have a regular table at some Cuban hotspot club. That alone costs big bucks. Definitely don't seem to do business old-school ways in offices, at restaurants, or whatever like I used to do." He chuckled.

She felt a little less uneasy at his outlook toward this meeting. As he went over the idea of offering the private client deal, she felt more comfortable with the upcoming meeting and confident she could get Alajandro and Toro to accept this deal. In fact, she had a feeling they would be thrilled.

"So good luck tonight. Can't wait to hear the good news tomorrow of a successful contract."

She walked out feeling numb and enthusiastic. She could do this. She could go out to dinner, discuss the business, and dance a little. She loved dancing and was very good at Latin and Brazilian dancing, which she knew was a great night at Club Magique. Knowing the owner's girlfriend was going to be a plus. She needed to call Caprice and ask that Morano, Angelo, or Vito call her.

* * * *

The business meeting at Club Magique finally came to an end.

"Well, that went better than expected," Mateus said to Major, Morano, Sunny, Vinny, and Dominick. Solencio Monteith and Tudoro Garlitto just exited the room.

"I didn't think there would be any problems. Everyone wants to make money. As long as you're willing to give a fair cut to those assisting, then all is good," Dominick said to them.

"What about Tudoro's concerns about the Torres family and stepping on their toes?" Morano asked.

"I don't foresee it as a problem because there's plenty of room for everyone to make money here. Nothing that stated Calvarro owns the cigar and import and exporting businesses across the US. There's enough money to be made by all," Mateus said.

"I don't like Calvarro or his ways of negotiating. They're a violent group of people, all of them. You know how I feel about Miami Cortez and those vicious gangbangers he uses," Dominick said.

"He's lucky that the order came down for you not to take him out, Dominick. Miami knows that. He won't fuck with you, or us, never mind Dmitri Sanclare," Mateus said to him.

"We're still more powerful than they are and have territorial rights. He wants to get pissed off? Then he can start back paying on all the business we've allowed him to reap the benefits from all these years. Fedarro and Collin don't give a fuck, either, about whether Calvarro gets pissed off at our families joining forces and making money. Like we mentioned earlier, he wasn't exactly jumping on board to assist when Rayanna was missing. Calvarro, as well as at least a dozen other assholes, thought that Puento was going to succeed in destroying Dmitri and us. So fuck him," Major stated.

"Agreed, but you still need to play nice. All our paths cross on a regular basis," Sunny said.

Dominick looked down at his cell phone as they were all preparing to leave the room. He walked over toward the balcony and the privacy window. From the club, it looked like mirrors, but from up here, he could see everything. His eyes landed on the front entryway and Giada. She looked incredible. She wore a very tight dark-blue dress that hugged her breasts and waist and then flared all around her hips like a skirt, and even from here, he could see every curve of her body and how short that skirt was with her wearing very high heels. She fit right in with the other women coming in to dance the Latin dances and even take lessons. He knew she knew how to dance. His cousin, Andreas, and his brother, Giuseppe, had witnessed her sexy dance moves with her friends. She gained a lot of attention, and he wondered who she was here with. That jealous feeling consumed him.

"What are you looking at?" Major asked, joining him. He whistled. "Damn, Giada looks good. I wonder if she's meeting the ladies here tonight. It is Latin night, right, Morano?"

"It is, and she called earlier today to reserve a private booth for dinner and then a spot up by the dance floor and bar for three people," Morano told them.

Dominick felt his fingers clench into fists by his side as he watched two men show up, kiss her hello, and guide her through the entryway as one of the hosts brought them toward the dining area. Both men had a hold on her and looked pleased.

"Who are the two guys?" Mateus asked Morano.

"I don't know. I never heard of them before, but they called before her and asked for a private table, and then Giada let me know it was friends of hers and that she wanted to impress them. Caprice knew nothing about them."

Dominick looked toward them, ready to leave and find out who the assholes were.

"You look pissed," Mateus stated to him.

"Do I?" he replied sarcastically.

"Hey, do you want us to find out who they are?" Morano asked, pulling out his phone.

"No. I'll take care of it." Dominick headed out of the room. He pulled out his cell phone. Brew had been the one who'd spotted her and texted him. He let Brew know that he was going to meet him by the bar.

It wasn't difficult to bump into them. Dominick was good at this type of stuff, but he felt as though his jealousy and anger could make him not come across so calm and collective. It was too late when Giada's eyes landed on him just as the host brought her and the two pretty boys, young fashionably dressed dicks, to their table.

"Giada." He glanced at the two men and back at her.

"Dominick, how are you? What are you doing here?" she asked.

He stepped closer and pulled her into a hug. He slid his hand along her waist to her ass, grazing it so the two men could see. He kissed her neck, not her cheek, and she tightened. He pulled back, and she was flushed, and as he looked her over close up, his cock came to full attention. The woman was fucking gorgeous, sexy, and feminine.

One of the men cleared his throat as he stared at her body, at the way the top didn't show off any cleavage but hugged her large breasts so well that it actually looked more sexy and classy like this than showing her breasts pouring from the top.

"So what are you doing here?" she asked.

"Just business, and you? Who are your friends?" he asked and saw how her facial expression changed when he said business. He wondered if Giuseppe was right and that maybe Giada was pretending to not like them and pushing them away because of their professions.

"These are friends of mine."

The one guy looked at her and smiled like that label pleased him, but it also seemed as if it was unexpected. Was she pretending these guys were friends or more than friends to make him step back and not pursue her? She was out of her mind. He, his cousin, and his brother hadn't even begun to pursue her.

"Alajandro Frane and Toro Miguel."

When she introduced them, Toro placed an arm around her waist and pulled her close as he shook Dominick's hand. The sight made Dominick put his hands on his hips, showing his firearm, which both men saw but didn't react to. That led him to more questions.

"You meeting your friends here for the Latin dancing later?" Dominick asked her, trying to remain calm seeing this guy, who appeared to be Hispanic, with his arm around her waist. She was petite and had a narrow waist, but her ass pushed out, and the guy's hand was pretty fucking close to that ass. He maintained his cool demeanor, but inside, he wanted to rip the motherfucker to pieces for having his hands on Giada.

"Oh, I don't know if they'll be coming. I made plans with Alajandro and Toro for the night, but I guess if they come here, I'll see them."

"Well, enjoy the night. I'm sure I'll see you later," he said, making her know that he wasn't going to leave or be far, let her think about that while she pretended to not have feelings for him, Giuseppe, and Andreas. Dominick then looked at the two guys one more time. He walked away, took out his cell phone, and texted the names of the two men to Brew. He would find out who the men were and what their interest was in Giada before he left the club.

* * * *

Giada was still trying to get over the effects on her body and mind after seeing Dominick and. of course, his seeing her with Alajandro and Toro. Who actually turned out to be so nice and charismatic that she was enjoying this business dinner. They ate and talked about the company and their investments in the cigar business and about how profitable things have been. She was impressed with their advertising and how they turned a handful of storefronts into dozens of storefronts.

"So, basically, the two of you were born in Cuba and then came here and started this business on your own?" she asked and took a sip of chardonnay from her glass.

Toro was staring at her lips while Alajandro placed his arm over the back of her chair. Both men had moved closer and closer to her as the music got louder and the place became more crowded. Club Magique always packed them in.

"We have relatives back in Cuba and Brazil who initially funded our dreams and business venture," Alajandro told her.

"Which we paid back immediately and gave us such a sense of accomplishment," Toro told her and stroked her arm.

She smiled softly. "That is impressive, and I'm certain the family is proud of both of you. Tell me, do you get to visit your family, or do they come here to visit you?"

"We invite them to come often. We usually have to buy out a couple of floors of the Grand Hotel, but it's well worth it to spoil them," Toro told her.

"Our penthouse isn't big enough to have them all stay there. Plus, we prefer to keep the penthouse private. We don't ever invite anyone over or host parties there," Alajandro said and gazed over her body.

She could sense the mood changing here from business to personal, and she wasn't sure how she felt. She definitely was attracted to both men, who were gorgeous, sexy, and definitely well-off businessmen, but in the back of her head, she thought about Dominick being here. She felt guilty, and it was stupid. She knew she couldn't get involved with him, Giuseppe, and Andreas. She just couldn't. But these men, businessmen, were safer to be with.

"How about you, Giada? Any family?" Alajandro asked her.

"Actually just an uncle, but we aren't close."

He stroked her knee. "That's a shame. We have a very large family. They would love you, for sure," Toro told her, holding her gaze.

She gave a soft smile but found his comment a little too much. She changed the subject back to business. "So what do you think about the option of being a private customer at Saks and Cain as I explained earlier?"

Both men eased back into their seats. "We appreciate you going to bat for us and trying to negotiate better terms. I, for one, think it's a great option and makes me feel like a personal touch is being offered here," Alajandro said to her and licked his lower lip after he said *personal touch.*

Oh boy was he a flirt and then some. She looked at Toro.

He smiled at her. "I think once we thoroughly have you checked out, we can commit fully to the deal."

She didn't quite think he meant fully checked out with his security. "Great." She looked away. She couldn't help but look around them. Maybe it was time to head upstairs to the bar and dance floors. "Should we walk around a bit and head upstairs? I need to use the ladies' room, and I know both of you couldn't wait to see the people dancing."

Alajandro nodded and winked at her. "We were hoping that you would dance with us. I bet you're a very seductive dancer, Giada."

They stood, and he placed a hand on her lower back. She stared up into his dark-brown eyes and didn't know how to respond. Toro pressed up against her back and placed a hand on her waist on the other side.

"I, for one, can't wait to see your moves."

He stroked her hip, and then Alajandro took her hand, and they walked away from the dining area and toward the bathrooms. Now she was nervous, especially as she walked with the men upstairs a few minutes later and into the crowded bar and dance floor. When she saw Dominick, Brew, Logic, and Turbo talking with Don and Clemenza Costanza, she really felt uncomfortable.

Turbo saw her, smiled, and made a face as if he was annoyed by seeing her with two other men. Did all their friends, the security guys, and everyone they knew think that she belonged to Dominick, Giuseppe, and Andreas already and that it was a done deal? She tightened up, and then Toro pressed up against her back and had his hand on her hip, sliding it up and down her upper hip and thigh as Alajandro led her to a table reserved for them. It was a high bar stool and three chairs by the back wall and, unfortunately, gave her a clear line of sight of the men she didn't want to see.

"What would you like to drink?" Toro asked her as a server immediately approached.

"Whatever you guys are having," she said, not really paying attention despite the cool music and how instantly she felt like dancing.

"Patrón," Toro told the server.

They watched the people dancing to the music and how some really could do the Latin, Brazilian moves and others couldn't. When the drinks came, they made a toast.

"To business and to pleasure," Alajandro said to her.

Both he and Toro eyed her over with interest. They all clicked glasses and did the shot. Toro asked for another round, but she knew she wasn't going to get drunk with these men or she would wind up in a heap of trouble. When the server approached with the next round, Giada asked for a club soda.

Toro rubbed her back and then her hip again. It seemed he and Alajandro really liked touching her hips.

"You feeling okay?" he asked her, his lips nearly touching her ear.

She looked up at him. "I'm good. I'm just not a heavy drinker. Plus, this is business."

Alajandro squinted at her as if her comment upset him, but then Toro was pulling her onto the dance floor. She couldn't help but laugh until the man began to move his hips like a pro and she realized that he and Alajandro were good dancers. As she got into the music and the beat, he would touch her hips, pull her close, and then step back, sliding his palms over her, just grazing her ass. It was sexy, and she would be lying if she said these men didn't make her feel sexy and desirable. When Alajandro joined them and took position behind her, the music slowed a little, and it was a sexy Brazilian number she knew how to move to. It got hot fast, and as people danced around them, it was almost competitive between couples and multiple couples dancing.

Somehow the three of them wound up in the center of a circle with the crowd cheering and the music going into a faster beat before a very slow beat. It was the kind of song to move your hips to and slither up and down, shaking your rear and then using a lot of arm movements and hips. It was beyond dirty dancing, and the roar and cheers of the crowd she was gaining everyone's attention. Alajandro and Toro gave her the spotlight, and she danced solo in the center of the circle, showing off her moves. She did this often with her girlfriends, and it usually led to guys hitting on them big time afterward. She had a funny feeling in her gut and wondered if Alajandro and Toro hit on her, would she accept their advances. They were super-good-looking, muscular, and sexy and had good jobs. More her speed than…she shook the thoughts from her head, getting upset that she'd thought about Dominick, Andreas, and Giuseppe.

Then as the music gained a little more speed, Alajandro and Toro joined her again. When the song ended, everyone was clapping and cheering for her, and Toro and Alajandro both pressed her between them, kissing her cheeks and holding on to her in a possessive manner. She looked away, feeling embarrassed a little, and locked gazes with a very angry-looking Dominick, along with several other pissed-off friends of his. She quickly turned away, and Toro and Alajandro took her hand and led her back to the table.

* * * *

Dominick couldn't take this shit. Thank God he didn't call Andreas and Giuseppe or those two men Giada was with would be beaten and bloody by now.

"Holy shit, does she know how to dance. Fuck," he heard Covan say.

The other men were making comments, as well, and it just aggravated him more. When he saw Giada get up and head to the ladies' room, he planned on following her.

"Keep eyes on those two assholes," he told Brew, who nodded and continued staring.

One look at the two men and he saw them smiling, watching Giada's ass as she walked away, and then nodding to one another, whispering like they were pleased as shit she was with them. She shouldn't be. They eased back in their seats, drank their drinks, and looked at the dance floor.

"I'll be back," he said to the guys.

"Want us to get rid of them?" Clemenza asked very seriously. There was no doubt that his friend would do that for him. He shook his head.

As he headed toward the hallways where the bathrooms were, he spotted Giada talking to two women who were complimenting her dancing as well as the two good-looking men she was with. The women passed him, and Giada looked up at him and stopped short.

He was pissed off. His chest was tight. He was flexing and not even on purpose. He'd never felt like this before. He stared at her sexy body, her full breasts pushing against the top of her tight dress, and her flared skirt and remembered how, when she danced, the material bounced against her thighs and lifted, teasing them, making him and others hope to see a glimpse of skin and ass. It was fucking hot and torturous to watch. It didn't help that people were recording her with their phones, including Brew, who would send it to him and then Andreas and Giuseppe later on.

She lowered her eyes and went to pass, and he gripped her upper arm and pulled her back. "What the fuck?" he asked her, not knowing what the hell to say, and those were the first words that shot from his mouth.

She narrowed her eyes at him. "Dominick, let go of my arm."

He pressed her up against the wall, keeping one arm above her head and his other hand against her waist and the wall. She stared up at him. She was feminine, sexy, and smelled incredible.

"Who the fuck are those guys? You're not seeing them, are you?" he asked, the words hurting his heart as he asked. Holy shit, this sucked.

"It really isn't any of your business."

She went to move, and he pressed his hand against her hip and stared down at her with a serious expression. "The hell it isn't. You know how we feel about you. Why are you pushing us away? Is this a game to fucking make us not pursue you?" he asked.

She opened her mouth to speak. Then it seemed as if she changed her mind. "They're friends, and it's business."

"Business?" he asked, squinting at her.

"Yes, tonight was a business dinner and a getting-to-know-one-another because of business things and confidential circumstances that I am not—and do not need to—going to share with you, Dominick. I need to get back." She went to move.

He leaned closer, inhaled her scent. The perfume, the shampoo, were addicting. He slid his hand up her hip and ribs. "Why the hell were you dancing so sexy with them if it was business?"

"It's how the song went and how the Latin Brazilian dance goes."

He took a few unsteady breaths and stared down into her gorgeous blue eyes. The woman was fucking hot. He inched his lips closer, and she pressed her palms to his chest.

"Dominick, don't. Nothing is going to happen between us. It will never work. I told you that."

"You're wrong. How can it not work when this feels so right?"

"You're all wrong for me. I don't want all the drama, the danger and violence, and the control and all the worrying. I can go on and on about all the things that make it impossible."

"I don't believe any of it. We protect what's ours. Don't you realize that?" he asked and pulled her into an embrace and then up against the wall. He kissed her chin, her neck, and she turned to the side, giving him better access to her skin.

"You feel it, baby. I know you do," he whispered, easing his palm along her ass and his other palm up her back. When he squeezed her ass, she tightened up and gripped his shoulders.

"Dominick, please. I can't handle it. I don't date. Really, this is business, and I need to get back."

As he eased away, inhaling her scent one more time, he narrowed his eyes at her, looking down, feeling protective and possessive of her. "If they try anything, you—"

She shook her head. "They won't. It's business."

"Not in their eyes. They want you."

And as she stepped from his hold and he turned to watch her walk away, he saw the one guy standing there. Brew was right behind the guy, but the guy didn't even know it. He narrowed his eyes at Dominick and looked down at Giada.

"Is everything okay? Is that guy bothering you?" he asked her.

Bothering her? You fucking dick. She's mine.

Giada looked back at him, and then she wrapped her arm around the guy's arm. "He's a good friend. That's all. Come on. One more drink?"

"The night is young, gorgeous, and I would love to see you strut your stuff on the dance floor with Alajandro and me," he said to her, and they headed out of the hallway.

The guy had the fucking nerve to look back toward Dominick as though he had the upper hand. Dominick had his hands on his hips and was breathing through his nostrils. What the fuck was he going to do about this? Fuck.

Chapter 4

Giada was in her office working out the details for the contracts for Alajandro and Toro. Her bosses, both Davis and Monterro, said they'd received calls from Alajandro and Toro about her professionalism and business sense and they felt confident in working with Saks & Cain for their banking needs. She just needed to meet them today at their office to be interviewed by their security person, and afterward, they wanted to take her to dinner.

She wanted to decline, but she knew she couldn't and needed to play nice, despite not wanting them to think there could be more between them. As much as she enjoyed spending time with them, Dominick's reaction stood out in her mind, and a guilty feeling consumed her. She wouldn't go out with Dominick, Giuseppe, and Andreas and allow her lust and desires make her make a huge mistake. But her mind kept going back to the look in Dominick's eyes, the feel of his hands on her body, his hand squeezing her ass, and his lips against her neck. She felt heated, aroused, and needy like nothing before.

That upset her even more so because she was trying to keep them away. She didn't want to date anyone, to be intimate with anyone. Not after Jimmy. She just wasn't over her soldier and losing him. Then last night, while she lay in bed thinking about Dominick, Giuseppe, and Andreas, she felt as though they made her feel things even Jimmy hadn't, and that was wrong. It wasn't right or respectful to Jimmy and what they'd shared. Those thoughts had her swearing to herself to not let her guard down or open her heart up to the dangers of made men.

She was preparing to leave for that appointment soon when her cell phone rang. Glancing at the caller ID, she saw it was Bella.

"Hello?" she asked smiling, always loving to hear from Bella.

"Hot damn, woman. You're like famous."

"What?" she asked, not knowing what she was talking about.

"Didn't you hear from Fina or Donata?"

"No. Why would I?"

"Um, your video is all over YouTube. It has like fifty thousand hits and counting."

"What video? What are you talking about?"

"Oh my God, you mean you didn't realize you were being recorded? Last night at Club Magique, multiple people recorded you, but one guy had the perfect angle, and holy shit, you looked amazing, Giada—like sexy hot, even I was blushing and fanning myself. Then when those two good-looking gods started dancing with you, sandwiching you, holy shit. Who are they? More important, what the hell happened between you and Dominick? I heard he was fuming mad and still is."

"Oh God, how do you know all this? What the heck?" Giada felt her cheeks warm as she looked through the window in her office and out toward Julia. If her bosses saw that video, they might not be too pleased with her. She thought about how she'd danced with Alajandro and Toro. It wasn't too sexy and did go along with the Latin music. "Shit. How much of the video shows me and the two guys?"

"Not much. Most of the copies are of your solo in the middle of the dance floor. You should be on stage with moves like that. Your hips were in perfect sync to the beat of music."

"Yikes."

"So who are the guys?"

"Businessmen I was having dinner with."

"Business? Honey, they were so into you, and I noticed that they didn't take advantage of the situation and touch your ass. They kept their hands on your hips or in the air."

"How the hell could you see all that?"

"I watched the video like a dozen-plus times. So did Mateus and Major. Now they want me to dance for them like that. I'll need pointers from you."

"Oh God." Giada lowered her head to her desk. Her heart was racing, and she felt so nervous. She hoped Alajandro and Toro hadn't heard about the video. Shit.

"Start talking," Bella said.

Giada looked at the time. "I'll have to talk on the way out of my office. I have a business meeting then dinner."

"With the two hotties?"

"Yes." She chuckled.

"Damn, woman. You are playing with fire. I mean you like these men? Like more than Dominick, Andreas, and Giuseppe?"

"Bella." Then she asked her to hold on while she said goodbye to Julia and handed her some documents to copy and save.

She got into the elevator and started telling Bella about what had happened.

"Oh man, I couldn't even imagine Dominick that pissed. He had you pressed up against the wall like that, and you didn't lose your mind and kiss him?"

"Bella, we've been over this before. You know I don't want this. I can't handle it. The worrying, the violence, and then the fears. They're made men, Andreas is retired military and a made man. It's too much."

"Honey, we can't help who we fall in love with."

"In love?" She shook her head, and immediately Giada's belly and heart ached. She wanted to cry. She needed to be strong. "No, Bella. It would be lust and nothing more. I would regret it. I haven't been with anyone since Jimmy."

"Well, there you go. It's time to move on. Perhaps if you did, then it would be easier to not make so many excuses as to why you can't date anyone."

"I'm not ready."

"How do you know?"

"I just do."

"It's okay to be afraid to take a chance. I know Jimmy was the only man you were ever with, and you dated for years and talked about getting married and all. It has to be so hard to get past it all, but Jimmy would want you to be happy and not alone."

"I'm not alone."

"When you aren't with the girls, with all of us, you are alone."

"I choose to be. Plus, work is so crazy, especially right now. I'm up for this new position. I'm going to be the liaison between the company and potential high-end clients. It means schmoozing them, dinners, lunches, conversation."

"Sexy dancing?" Bella asked and chuckled.

"That just kind of happened. It also helped that both men are of Latin descent."

"Oh hot tamales. I thought you preferred Italian?" Bella teased.

"Very funny," Giada said.

Bella snickered. "Are you going to meet up with us at Club X after the boxing match Friday night as we all planned?"

"Um…"

"Oh come on. You aren't seriously going to avoid their club, are you?"

"Well, I don't think it's a good idea, and especially if Dominick was so angry. I don't want it to look like I'm playing some sort of game here. I really need to keep my distance. I'm assuming that they'll be at the boxing match."

"Of course they will be, and we have great seats, too. Listen, you can hang with the guys and me."

"I'll let you know. I have a busy week and this deal to seal, plus another client to meet Thursday."

"Okay, but I am going to be seriously pissed if you duck out on us. Caprice needs us there for moral support. She hates when Angelo gets in the ring to fight, especially after he beat the crap out of the Irishman. Now this guy, Finarro Lupez, is some crazy Cuban dude. He's got some major backing from big-shot money guys Mateus and Major know. Anyway, we'll hold a seat as long as we can. So let me know by Thursday."

"Okay, will do."

Giada got into the cab and headed to Alajandro and Toro's business a few blocks away. She smoothed her hands down her thighs. The pencil-tight dress hugged her figure and landed right above her knees. It was classy, professional, and a little sexy, especially with the high heels. She wasn't sure what to expect with this investigation by their security personnel. Her boss had said running her through the system, fingerprinting, background checks, and personal questions. She swallowed hard. If she were a criminal or had done anything in her life that she felt embarrassed about, she would be in for one hell of an afternoon.

* * * *

"They own cigar stores and importing and exporting companies throughout the United States and particularly here in New York," Brew said to Dominick, Giuseppe, and Andreas.

Andreas was looking at the YouTube video for the hundredth time, getting angrier and angrier.

"Legit or not?" Giuseppe asked, leaning back in the seat, looking calm and unaffected, but Andreas knew he wasn't.

Dominick was being a prick, Giuseppe was snappy, and well, he felt like hunting down these fuckers and taking them out. It was insane how jealous he felt.

"From what we gathered they look like they're legit, but we didn't dig too deep. Didn't want to send up any red flags," Brew said.

"We did find out that these guys, Alajandro and Toro, are transferring accounts from some banks in Florida to Saks and Cain, which indicates those accounts to be in the hundreds of thousands or more. Saks and Cain usually only deal in high-end business securities," Train said.

"Yes, and it appears that Giada's position puts her into the spot as negotiator for these accounts, along with her boss, a Monterro Spain," Royce said.

"What do you have on him?" Dominick asked.

"We didn't investigate him," Train said to Dominick.

"Do you think that's necessary?" Giuseppe asked.

"It wouldn't hurt, but for now let's not. The information we wanted was about these two guys who were with her last night. There was something about them, about the one guy who looked at me when I had her in the hallway. The way he placed his hand on her hip in a possessive manner, he knew I was carrying, saw my piece, had to figure out I was the real deal, and he didn't bat an eye, was confident, not just being chivalrous. My gut says there's more," Dominick said.

"Maybe he liked her so much he just reacted and didn't think. It isn't like you came out and showed him the piece and threatened him," Train said to him.

"No, it was more," Dominick added.

"She did look incredible last night, and that video, it's all over the place," Brew added.

Andreas clenched his teeth. "We need to see her, to talk to her. If these two guys are trouble or up to no good, then I'm not going to stand by and watch her get hurt just because she's fighting us."

"I agree. If what she told you was true, Dominick, and she doesn't think she can handle the violence and the dangers our lives and professions entail, then she sure as shit wouldn't want to be getting involved with these two Cuban assholes if they're up to no good," Giuseppe said.

"That would be fucked up. Running from you three only to wind up involved with men who could hurt her or be involved with criminal activities. Might I suggest we dig a little further? Perhaps put someone on their business or them to see who they interact with?" Royce added.

"I'm hesitant to do that just yet," Dominick stated.

"That's because she made her fears known to you, and by having these men followed and investigated, it proves her fears are legit. That you guys are involved in things and capable of things she doesn't think she can handle. It's understandable, boss, but it's better to be smart and figure out who these men are quickly," Royce added.

"We'll think about it." Giuseppe exchanged looks with Dominick and Andreas.

"When can we see her?" Andreas asked in a hard tone.

Giuseppe and Dominick looked at him and didn't answer.

Royce cleared his throat. "I spoke with Antonio this morning. He said that Bella was on the phone with Giada and trying to get her to go to the fight Friday night, then to Club X afterward. She was saving her a seat and would know by Thursday if she would attend."

"Well then, I guess it will be Friday night. We'll see if we can persuade her to sit down and talk," Giuseppe said.

"You can talk. I'm too fucking pissed to be calm about this shit. Now, let's move on to business. The first transactions took place last night, and everything went smoothly. If the importing and deliveries go this smooth, we're going to make a nice side profit along with the Costanzas, the Fiorres, and Dmitri. Our only issue was a few people gave a little bit of a hard time. They were loyal to Calvarro and thought he had priority over the product. They were dealt with accordingly to send a clear message, correct, Royce?" Dominick said.

"Yes. We're ready for any further bumps or interference," Royce said

"Good."

Chapter 5

"Who the fuck do they think they are? First, they'll start with little dips into our money pot, and then they'll take over. This is bullshit and has the potential for disaster. We could lose our gold mine. Ours," Calvarro Torres said to the group of men sitting in the meeting room.

"What do we do? Those are three major organized-crime families with pull and power we don't have here in the States," Loppo said to him.

"We have pull and power. We have resources that have allowed us to get away with bringing in the illegal goods without problem or detection. Dmitri Sanclare, the Costanzas, the Fiorres and the Coglonies don't have what we have. The smartest move was investing in the small cigar businesses with my cousin's kid Alajandro and his friend Toro. With more than fifty storefronts and other strip malls, we have our cover and locations to hide our goods. These men don't have that," Calvarro told them all.

"How are they coming along with getting those bank accounts set up? We need places to hide the money that the feds and cops won't get wind of," Louis Bronnos, owner of the club Cha Cha Cabana, asked. He, too, had an investment in this operation and didn't want to lose money to these other families.

"They are scheduled to meet the representative here today in about thirty minutes," Loppo said to them.

"A woman?" Calvarro asked.

Loppo smiled. "A very attractive woman with hidden talents." He smirked.

Two of the other security guys smiled.

"What do you mean?" Calvarro asked. Then he listened to them explain about the business meeting at Club Magique, owned by the Fiorre family; how it was Latin dance night; and how the woman was amazing.

"There's a video on YouTube," one of the others told him.

"I hope they're thinking with the right heads. We need to be careful," Calvarro stated.

"Take a look at the video or, better yet, stick around and meet her. She's due here momentarily, and Alajandro and Toro can't wait," one of the security guys, Apponte, said to him.

"Okay, let's handle the other aspects of business, including the deliveries set for tonight. I need a few of you working on making sure Costanza, Fiorre, and Sanclare do not get a hold of our other distributors. Be ready to negotiate terms and make it so that they don't stray. We start losing our connections, and we'll be shoved out, and these fuckers will take over what belongs to us. I mean what the fuck?" Calvarro stated in annoyance.

"We could ask for a sit-down to discuss this business. Come up with some sort of agreement with them," Louis Bronnos suggested.

"Seriously, Louis, you think that sit-down would end up in our favor and not theirs? They'll put the pressure on, make their threats, and we will end up with a twenty percent cut of what we've been making a seventy-five percent profit on. No fucking way am I meeting with them. No fucking way," Calvarro stated firmly.

The others nodded, and everyone started to leave the room.

A few minutes later, as Calvarro headed out of the meeting room with Loppo and Apponte, his two main security guys, his eyes landed on the backside of one very sexy woman with long, wavy black hair that reached her mid-back. She wore a tight dress that accentuated her toned thighs, and, holy shit, when she turned around with Alajandro and he locked his gaze on a gorgeous face, ocean-blue eyes, full lips, and a sweet, sensual smile, his heart began to race. No wonder his cousin and his friend were enthralled with this woman. She was perfection.

"Calvarro, great timing. We would like you to meet Giada Slane. She's the representative from Saks and Cain."

Calvarro immediately reached out his hand and gave the woman a smile and wink. "Gorgeous young woman, and obviously very intelligent, as well, to be working at Saks and Cain," he said, and she blushed. She was precious indeed.

She pulled her hand back, and he realized he was staring at her and had held her hand a little too long.

"So what are we up to today?" he asked.

"Loppo is going to do the final security clearance with Giada, and then we're off to dinner. Would you like to join us?" Toro asked, obviously noticing Calvarro's interest.

"I have other plans but would love to get to know Giada since she'll be privy to personal information about the businesses. How about Friday night, you bring her to the event? I'll have Loppo get another three seats first row."

"Great. We'll tell her all about it over dinner."

He shook her hand good-bye, and he and Loppo walked away a moment. "Get everything you can on her."

Loppo smiled. "Your cousin and his buddy are very into her."

"I'm sure they are, but this is business. She'll be privy to money transactions and could be nosey and ask questions. We'll need to ensure she knows who is in charge."

"Got it."

"Good, and make sure they get her to come to the fight."

"Will do." Loppo headed back to interview Giada.

* * * *

Giada was tired after all the questions from Loppo, a very hard, intimidating man who headed security for corporate headquarters. She didn't like the personal questions he asked, but it did give her the opportunity to let him, Alajandro, and Toro know that she didn't date and why. She felt a bit uncomfortable, to say the least, but when they were finally finished, even Loppo smiled at her.

"I know it probably seemed overkill, but you must understand that men in our positions and with the money we make have to be cautious. There always seems to be people trying to swindle us or steal," Alajandro stated.

"I understand, and well, as uncomfortable as this was, and a first for me, I can understand all your concerns. Just keep in mind that I'm only going to be checking the account a few times a year, and in your presence. You have control over the passwords and everything like that. So really, you maintain the upper hand. No matter who checks out the accounts to bill them accordingly, they sign a confidentiality agreement. The penalties to an employee who breaks that contract of confidentiality are extreme to say the least. Their life would be over."

Alajandro smiled.

"We read that detailed confidentiality contract, and it is definitely in favor of the client. We respect that and the terms," Toro told her.

"So you worked for Saks and Cain for a few years now. How do you see the security aspect changing for the better? Are they upgrading their system anytime soon?" Loppo asked.

"Well, from my understanding, there are constantly changes taking place on the manual level, you know with employees and the hands-on aspect. I do believe that a newer, more advanced system has been in the works for the better part of a year. The changes will be slow and steady, nothing abrupt that can cause any glitches. The vaults, the security cabinets where people have their actual money stored, won't change. It's top notch, and no new technology is going to improve that."

"Why do you think that when there are so many new, advanced systems being used?" Loppo asked her.

"I think because many of these new systems are too reliable on outside sources and too many variables need to be in sync. The ones operated by computer systems alone could be hacked into, have glitches, or even loss of data. Old-school technology, keeping hard records on file as well as detached storage data, ensures no mistakes are made. I mean could you imagine if we used computer technology solely to keep track of the accounts and the monies in them, and then it gets hacked or there's a malfunction? Your five hundred thousand could become fifty thousand with a zero being left off or, worse, money into another person's account. That's extreme, I know, but not a chance any reputable bank will be willing to take. This idea of high-end security vaults, geared toward individuals like yourselves who want their money to be safe, secured, accessible but also private, is fantastic."

"You've already sold us on the company, Giada, but your enthusiasm is appreciated," Toro said to her.

She smiled. "I enjoy working for the company. It's gotten me through some tough times."

"Well, I'll leave the three of you alone and head out. It was a pleasure meeting you, Miss Slane," Loppo said and shook her hand.

"Thank you," she said, and then Loppo left the room.

She stood there looking at both Alajandro and Toro, who leaned against the desk. Alajandro stepped closer and took her hand.

"We're sorry if Loppo was a bit intrusive. It was necessary, but also let us in on who you are personally, and that gives us peace of mind."

"It's okay. I agreed, and now that part is over."

"Yes, and now we have you all to ourselves for a relaxing, enjoyable dinner to celebrate a new beginning in business together," Toro added, stepping closer, too. She looked up at both men, feeling an attraction yet an invisible force field that kept her from accepting the attraction. She just wasn't ready for anything.

"Shall we head out? It's later than we planned," Toro said to her.

"Sure. Thank you for the invite."

"Well, we're hoping to be friends, Giada—close ones." Alajandro guided her from the office with a hand at her hip.

* * * *

"So what you're saying is that Calvarro is your mom's cousin and he was the one to front you the money to start your own business?" Giada asked then took a sip of wine.

Alajandro couldn't help but stare at her lips and wonder what she tasted like. He and Toro had been over it so many times—the way she made them feel, how sexy and feminine she was. She'd made it clear that she didn't date because of the loss of her boyfriend, a man who'd served in the military. Women loved men in uniform, and it kind of pissed him off that she was in love with a man and two years later still didn't date. She was sweet, almost pure, and he got the feeling that this man she had been with had been her only lover. She was practically a virgin.

"Yes, without his financial and supportive backing, Toro and I wouldn't have succeeded in achieving our dreams."

"That is amazing, and he must be so proud. So is he involved in the businesses too?" she asked.

"Not really. He always asks about how we are doing. Sometimes we feel compelled to give him part of our earnings, but he declines. Has his set of businesses. I wonder if that's why he asked for you to attend the event on Friday evening." Alajandro sipped the wine. Dinner had been exceptional, and the sweet woman had tried to pay for the meal.

"What event?" she asked.

"A boxing match downtown that is bringing in a lot of attention. We have seats all arranged for us, you included, and then we can hit one of the clubs afterward," Toro told her.

"Oh, I was actually supposed to get together with friends to see that fight and to go to Club X afterward."

"Really? Your girlfriends like to watch boxing matches?" Toro asked.

She chuckled. "Actually one of my girlfriends is dating one of the boxers."

"Which boxer?" Alajandro asked.

"Angelo Fiorre."

He couldn't believe this. She was friends with the girlfriend of the Fiorre brothers. They were a known family, very wealthy and powerful.

"We have money on him to win," Toro told her and then eased his arm over the back of her chair.

She glanced at him. "He's very good but doesn't fight too often. He picks and chooses, I guess."

"That's what we heard, but he's good enough. That's for sure," Toro said.

"So you'll go with us and sit with us?" Alajandro asked.

"I don't know. I kind of promised my friend I would sit with her."

"Knowing that the Fiorre brothers share the same woman, I'm certain that she won't be alone without you there." Toro couldn't help but feel excited that Giada might be interested in being shared by him and Toro. That would be a very fun night in bed.

"No, of course not, but there are a few of us single women hanging out with her and then afterward at the club. It's Friday night."

"Well, why don't we compromise? You watch the fight with us and then join your friends at the club afterward? That way we have time to spend together so you can meet Calvarro and see if he's interested in doing some business with you, as well."

"Okay," she said.

Alajandro smiled. "Shall we drive you home now?"

"I can grab a cab."

"Nonsense. We'll drive you."

They headed out of the restaurant and to the Range Rover.

When they arrived at her apartment building, Alajandro noticed the dirty looks he and Toro got from the security guard.

"Good evening, Giada. Is everything okay?" the guy asked.

"Sure thing, Donny. My friends are just walking me up, and they'll be right down."

The guard nodded and totally stared at them. One look at Toro and he could see that he'd picked up on it.

As they headed into the elevator, Alajandro felt compelled to make a move, so when they got out and she stood by her door, he pushed for more alone time. He reached out and stroked her cheek with the back of his knuckles. "How about you invite us in and we talk some more?"

She lowered her eyes, and Toro stepped closer to her and placed a hand on her hip. "It will be a good thing. The three of us," he said to her.

She swallowed hard. "I told you that I don't date."

Alajandro pulled her close, making her gasp. "Who said anything about dating?" He pressed his lips to hers. She seemed to like it until Toro joined in, kissing her neck and gripping her hair. As Alajandro pulled back, Giada looked scared.

"We shouldn't. It's not a good idea," she said.

"I think it's a great idea. We're attracted to you and you to us," Toro told her and kissed her neck some more.

"It's bad to mix business with pleasure."

"Not when you look this hot and we want you between us." Alajandro pressed closer, only for her to push against his chest.

"No. We can't. I'm sorry, but I don't date, and I don't sleep with clients. Please understand."

He was disappointed, but he knew this wasn't going to be his last attempt at kissing her, breaking down her defenses, and having her with Toro.

"We're disappointed," Toro said to her.

"Maybe we shouldn't get together Friday night then." She took out her keys.

Alajandro touched her hand. "Calvarro invited you, and he wants to talk. We'll work it out. We'll take our time. Maybe that's what you need." He stroked her cheek with his knuckles.

She nodded and opened her door. He thought of taking her anyway, of pushing her inside and making her their woman, but he didn't act on that desire. He would play the game and wait a little longer. She was that appealing. He just hoped his cousin wasn't thinking and wanting the same thing. If Calvarro was interested in Giada, then they would have no choice but to back off. He was the boss, the head of the Cuban family, and no one fucked with him, ever. Alajandro and Toro would be nothing if it hadn't been for Calvarro Torres. Nothing.

* * * *

Giada exhaled and leaned against the door to her apartment. She was out of her mind turning down two hot, sexy, perfect businessmen like Alajandro and Toro. Absolutely out of her mind. She could just imagine what Fina, Donata, Alda, Alessa, and the others would say when she told them what happened.

She pushed off the door and knew why she'd turned them down. First, she didn't do one-night stands or have sex with men, business or personal. Two years. Two years without sex, intimacy, and even as desperate as she sometimes felt to feel loved or get embraced, she couldn't let down the guard to do it. Her heart would instantly open up. She would read into what happened, maybe become clingy to a guy, and it would piss a man or men off. She knew that. Two, something held her back from letting go or even feeling as if she could let go with Alajandro and Toro. So what that they were fine, fine specimens of men. Jesus, were they super sexy, and those accents?

She plopped onto the couch and exhaled. She stared toward the window and the night. She thought of the Coglonie men. Of Dominick, which brought her to number three. If she were to lose her ever-loving mind, throw inhibition to the wind, and not worry about tomorrow, about the consequences of having sex again, then she would do it with them.

Tears stung her eyes. Bella was right. Giada was already in love with Andreas, Dominick, and Giuseppe.

"Damn it!" she exclaimed and slammed her fist down on the couch.

They were all wrong for her. All wrong. What was she thinking? Why them of all men, of all people? She met businessmen on a regular basis—good-looking ones, action-oriented ones, boring ones, conservative ones—you name it, and she met them. None did anything for her. None had her dreaming about them, imagining their touch, or imagining that it was their cocks inside of her body instead of her vibrator.

Heck, that thing wasn't even working anymore. It took the edge off, and that was about it.

She heard her cell phone buzz, and she reached for her bag, looking for a distraction from these thoughts. When she cleared the screen and saw the text message from Andreas, she felt as if her heart stopped beating for half a second.

Making sure that you're okay.

She typed back, *No, not okay. Come over.* But then she erased it. *I need you so badly I hurt.* She erased that, too. *Thank you for checking in. I think I'm okay. Maybe.*

She stared at that. Would he get concerned and come over?
Did she want him to?

Yes…no…I can't.

She erased her reply and put down her phone. It was better to not answer at all.

Chapter 6

Giada walked into the waiting room at her office Thursday to meet a new client. The second her eyes landed on the man she recognized him from a couple of weeks ago at Celia's. He squinted, and then a huge smile formed on his face.

"Mocha martini."

"Crown Royal," she countered, shaking his hand, and they both smiled.

The instant their hands touched she felt something. A spark of interest maybe? What were the chances of multiple men giving her this reaction in one week's time? Maybe she was just getting desperate to move past the walls and get on with a love life? To avoid feeling anything for the Coglonie men and really push them out of her life? Perhaps one man instead of multiple would make it easier to let down her guard and try intimacy again? This guy sure was attractive.

He stared at her. "This is starting off a hell of a lot better than I expected. It's Giada Slane, correct?"

She pushed her hair behind her shoulders. "Oh God, yes, sorry, and you are Emanuel Cortez?" she asked, remembering the name on the file her boss, Monterro, had given her. He was the one who'd put her in contact with this potential client.

"Yes."

"Great, well follow me into my office, and we can talk about your interests in Saks and Cain. Can I get you anything to drink? Water, coffee?" she asked as they passed by Julia, who stood and stared at Emanuel, practically drooling.

Emanuel smiled. "Julia, I'll be in a meeting with Mister Cortez. Can you hold all calls, please?"

"Yes, of course."

"Thank you." Giada motioned for Emanuel to enter her office. She closed the door, and he immediately took in the pictures she had on her bookshelf, one with her and Jimmy. Jimmy was in uniform, and she was wearing a pretty, sexy sundress. It was a week before he passed.

"Boyfriend?" he asked and looked at her, eyeing her body.

"He passed away a couple of years ago while serving."

He squinted at her. "So sorry for your loss."

"Thank you. So, Mister Spain hadn't really explained what your interests are in Saks and Cain. I'm assuming that you are looking to open some accounts and explore our services."

He moved closer to where she stood, and he paced his hands on his hips. The man dressed completely designer but not custom. So he had money but maybe not too much.

"Monterro is a character and highly recommended you to help me decide whether or not I'm interested in using this bank for the financial security of my money. I have a series of importing and exporting businesses in the US and abroad. I have other accounts overseas, but after a security breach at Waynes and Smith, let's just say I was concerned."

She leaned back against her desk and crossed her arms in front of her chest in a relaxed stance, despite how the butterflies wiggled in her belly. He even smelled good. "Rightfully so. It was a scare for them, and some customers' accounts were hacked into. In their defense, they did resolve everything very quickly, and any customers who suffered were taken care of."

He gave a soft smile and just stared at her a moment longer than what she thought was normal. She felt her cheeks warm, and then she straightened her shoulders.

"Interesting."

"What is interesting?" she asked him.

"That you didn't bad-mouth Waynes and Smith to promote your own bank here."

"Why would I? They are a reputable bank. Things happen that are out of our control."

"Fate you mean, Giada?" he asked, and then his expression toward her was flirty.

She swallowed hard. "Perhaps. So, what exactly are you interested in or want to learn more about?"

"Besides you? I suppose the securities you offer here. Package deals, charges, et cetera." He glanced at his watch.

She was shocked by his forwardness and how uncomfortable it made her feel.

"I'd like to set up a more detail-oriented meeting with you. Monterro mentioned your availability for next week, let's say Tuesday, my office at eleven?" he asked.

"I thought today's meeting was about asking questions and finding out information about the company and what we have to offer."

"Oh, it was going to be, but as I waited for you, I received a phone call from a business associate, and my schedule for this morning changed abruptly. I didn't want to be rude and reschedule, then leave. I'm glad I didn't, or I wouldn't have found out that the woman I was meeting turned out to be the same woman I couldn't stop thinking about last week when we met by chance. I'd say this could be very positive, Miss Slane." He reached out his hand for her to shake.

She did immediately, uncertain about this whole meeting thing, and when he took her hand and brought it to his lips, kissed the top, and held her gaze, she had a feeling this was going to get a little crazy fast.

"I'll have my secretary call yours and confirm the time and location. I look forward to our meeting. Fate is a very powerful power, indeed."

He walked out of her office, leaving her there feeling sort of dumbfounded and unsure what had just happened.

"Oh my God, who is he? He's drop-dead gorgeous and that accent? Wowzas." Julia placed her hand over her heart as she acted all dramatic.

"I have no idea really, but it seems I'll be meeting him at his office Tuesday to discuss his position as a potential client."

"I should have gone to graduate school. I wish I were better at math like you. You meet all the hot guys. I meet losers."

Giada chuckled. "You do not meet losers. Bradley was nice."

Julia rolled her eyes and placed her hands on her hips. "I was dating him for a week and went to watch a football game with him, and he asked me to fetch his beers from the refrigerator. Seriously?"

Julia walked out of Giada's office, and Giada chuckled, but then she thought about the hot guy. Her cell phone rang, and she looked at it. Fina was calling. "Hey, what's going on?"

"Not much. Just making sure you aren't going to be a no-show tomorrow night."

"What? No way. I can't wait to hang out with you ladies."

"Good because I hear there are going to be a lot of hot guys at Club X, especially after the match."

She couldn't resist telling Fina about Emanuel.

"Speaking of hot guys, remember Crown Royal from Celia's?"

"The gorgeous Latin guy with the accent? Older, sexy as sin, and drooling over you, who blew him off? Yup. I remember him."

"Well, he was here this morning—a potential new client."

"No way. Oh my God, Giada, you're getting a second chance," Fina said to her.

"I don't know about that."

"Oh brother. If you're going to blow off a guy like that, plus the two hotties you were doing the dirty with on the dance floor last week, I think you need to see a shrink. You've lost your freaking mind," Fina stated very seriously.

Giada laughed. "You seriously aren't attracted to any of these hot, wealthy men?"

"I wouldn't say that. It's just not like I'm super-attracted to them."

"Honey, why aren't you going after who you really want? You're practically in love with Dominick, Andreas, and Giuseppe. Just go for it and let the rest of us have a chance at these other hotties. You can't have them all," Fina teased.

"I am not in love with them."

"Sure you aren't. So you must be gay then and like women."

"What?"

"There's no other excuse. I mean, seriously, these men you meet who show interest are so fucking hot it would make a lesbian stray, and you're all blah about them."

"You're absolutely nuts, do you know that, Fina?"

"I'm nuts? You belong in the nut house pushing away all these sexy men. I think you do need Friday night to let go—hell, the whole weekend. Maybe we need a trip to Vegas."

Giada laughed louder. "On that note, I'm going back to work. I'll see you tomorrow night."

Giada ended the call and exhaled. Was she really losing her mind here? Was she being too cautious, too scared to date, to let another man touch her? She shook her head. Things were getting complicated quickly. She needed to focus on work. Work never brought her trouble. It took her away from complications and thoughts she wasn't ready to process. *Back to work. Now.*

* * * *

"Where is she?" Andreas asked Bella.

Bella exhaled. "Giada isn't sitting with us. She's meeting clients' here, but I do believe she's going to be at your club afterward, Andreas."

Andreas looked at Giuseppe and Dominick. They appeared disappointed, too.

"Those guys you checked out she was doing business with have a definite connection to Calvarro. Royce was right in what he found out this morning," Brew told them as he came up behind Giuseppe.

"What?" Andreas asked.

Brew nodded toward the entryway, and Andreas couldn't believe his eyes. Giada was walking in with not only the two dicks she'd dirty danced with the other night but also Calvarro Torres and his entourage.

"I'm going to say hello," Giuseppe stated calmly.

Andreas stood where he was, along with Dominick, Brew, Train, Major, and Morano.

Morano whispered to him. "It has to be business, and she more than likely doesn't have a clue as to who Calvarro is or what he's connected to."

"I would hope not," Dominick said, clenching his teeth.

Andreas looked over as Giuseppe said hello. They greeted him with smiles, but Giada looked uncomfortable. Giuseppe pulled her into an embrace and kissed her cheek but also ran his palm along her ass. She gripped his shoulders, and they locked gazes.

"What the hell did Giuseppe say to her?" Andreas asked.

Dominick grunted his words. "Stay the fuck away from these men. You belong to Coglonie, I hope."

Andreas felt his heart pounding. What the hell was she thinking?

* * * *

Giada was shocked when Giuseppe pulled her into his arms, kissed her neck, and whispered into her ear, "These are bad men you're with. You're safest with us. Be careful."

She was shocked, but then she felt his palm slide along her ass, and he purposely let Calvarro and the guys see. Was this some sort of a macho claim to her or what? She was a bit embarrassed. Now these men would think she'd slept with Giuseppe.

He remained holding her at his side. "Do you mind if I snag Giada a few minutes to say hello to her friend Caprice? She's a little nervous about her boyfriend fighting tonight?"

"It's up to Giada," Alajandro said, and she could tell that Calvarro didn't like his response but forced a fake smile and a nod.

"I'll be quick. That way we can talk before the fight starts," she said to Calvarro.

He gave her a wink. "Yes, make it quick, Giada. We have things to discuss." He eyed Giuseppe.

Giuseppe pulled her along with him, his grip tight on her waist.

"I'm going to trip if you keep walking this fast, Giuseppe."

He slowed down. "Do you have any idea who that guy is?"

His reprimand made her feel like a child. "He's a relative to the two men I'm working with."

"A relative?" he asked as he pulled her into a crowd with his brother, cousins, and Caprice.

She hugged Caprice hello and wished her luck. "Is Angelo nervous?"

"I don't think so. I'm the one freaking out."

"He'll do great. He's an excellent fighter, and you've watched him before." Giada felt the hands on her shoulders and then the warm breath against her neck.

"You should be sitting with us tonight, not Cuban fucking gangsters," Dominick stated firmly.

She turned to look at him as Morano pulled Caprice away from them. Their guards, Brew, Royce, and Logic, blocked the view from any prying eyes. Dominick moved her to the side hallway, and Andreas and Giuseppe came with him.

"Those are dangerous men you're hanging around with, baby. Dangerous. Why?" Dominick asked her.

She didn't know that they were part of the Cuban mafia or whatever. "I just met him the other day when I was working with Alajandro and Toro." She turned to look that way, but Dominick cupped her cheek and made her look way up into his eyes.

"Don't let them touch you and act like you belong to them. It's fucking bullshit." Dominick turned that way, but the guys' backs blocked the view.

"Don't, Dominick. We've been over this before. I don't belong to anyone." She saw the change in his eyes, a darkness she wasn't used to seeing. It unnerved her and, for some stupid reason, made her feminine parts go on alert. "I need to go." She went to move, but Andreas pulled her back.

"Just stay here with us. I'll tell them for you," Andreas stated.

He started to turn, but she grabbed his hand. "No. Don't do that. It's business and nothing more. I'm working with his cousins. Their mom is Calvarro's first cousin. Please, just let me get through the match, and then I'm done. I already told them I was meeting up with friends at Club X."

"No. I don't like it."

Andreas pulled her closer. She pressed her palm against his chest. He was so angry. All three of them were, and they wanted to protect her. She knew they were sincere, and she didn't know anything about Calvarro.

"Just trust me to handle this. It is business. I swear, Andreas, don't make a scene. It's work related, and after tonight, there really isn't a need to socialize with them."

"They want you," Giuseppe stated through clenched teeth.

She swallowed hard and glanced at him. He looked just as angry as Dominick. All three of these men were older, super-intense men. She was sort of afraid of their capabilities. She knew they would never hurt her, but they were capable of doing bad things when pushed. She understood that, could respect it to an extent, but not right now when she could lose her job over this.

"Don't push me or tell me what I'm doing or not doing." She slid out of Andreas's arms and stepped past Brew. She held on to his arm as she slid past then locked gazes with Alajandro and Toro, who were approaching, obviously looking for her.

She turned around, smiled, and waved at the guys. "I'll talk to Caprice later, after the match." She felt the arm go around her waist and hold her snuggly. Alajandro was now showing possession of her, and she didn't know how to react, especially as she saw Dominick narrow his eyes then turn away.

"Everything okay?" Alajandro asked her, turning her away from the men and making her feel less protected and more in danger.

She exhaled. She needed to be smart here. "My friends are upset that I'm not joining them for the match, but I'll see them later."

"The Coglonie men too?" Toro asked her.

She looked at him. "We're friends. That's all."

Alajandro stopped her, and Toro pressed up behind her. She was caught between them. Alajandro cupped her cheek and jaw and stared down into her eyes and then at her lips.

"You're important to them?" he asked and stroked her jaw.

He towered over her by a foot, and he was thick, solid, and fit. She stared up into his dark brown eyes. "All of them are important to me, too, especially Caprice's men and their cousins. They all have kind of taken the responsibility of looking out for the girls. You know, the single ones."

Toro caressed her hip then under her hair. She tightened up.

"Seems more like they want you in their bed," Toro stated.

"I don't date. You know that. So now that this is becoming uncomfortable, I think you should release me so we can sit down and talk business, like what Calvarro is interested in."

Alajandro glanced over his shoulder, and she could see where he was looking—right at Andreas, who stood by Brew watching her.

Alajandro stroked her jaw and let his thumb caress her lower lip as he stared down into her eyes. "I should kiss you right now and let them know that you're not interested."

She pulled back. "I thought we discussed this the other night. How I don't date and why."

He reached out to stroke her jaw. "Maybe you just need a little persuading."

She turned away from him. "No, I'm not interested, and if this is going to be a continuous problem, then perhaps we need to renegotiate who you have monitoring your accounts with Saks and Cain so we don't have further issues."

He pulled back and glared at her. "I'd hate for it to come to that over these men you call friends. I would also hate having to call your boss and say there may be a change in plans as to who we use for our banking needs."

Her heart hammered. If she lost this account, then she would surely lose her job.

"Why don't we let her think about that a little? Calvarro is waiting, and the first match already started," Toro stated, and then they escorted her to their seats.

Sure enough, they were down in front in great seats and diagonal to where her friends sat. She wouldn't look that way, especially not as Calvarro asked her to take a seat next to him so they could talk. When he placed his arm over the back of her seat and started whispering questions into her ear, she tightened up and wished she wasn't in this situation. Here she was trying to push away men who she thought were dangerous and too powerful and intimidating to be with and had wound up next to Cuban gangsters who were already trying to manipulate her and strong-arm her into compliance for whatever it was they were after. Knowing that they obviously knew the Coglonie men and the other families, and they didn't seem too happy to learn she was good friends with them, this was a dangerous situation, and she had to be smart and play it cool. Any other way could mean trouble.

* * * *

"So I understand that you're very good at your job, Giada, and will be taking on a new role in the company very soon," Calvarro said to her.

She wondered how he knew that. It was a conversation between herself and her bosses, Davis and Monterro.

"Ahh, was I not supposed to know that? Hmm, I guess you will learn that I'm a resourceful man, capable of many things."

She shivered from the look in his eyes and the way he leaned into her. He was a big man, not as tall as he was thick and slightly overweight. He had a wealthy look to him, though—designer dress shirt and jacket, black pants, expensive shoes, and a gold chain around his neck that peeked out from the collar of his shirt. His hair was slicked back and showed specks of gray at his temples. His dark-blue eyes bore into hers, and he inhaled.

"You smell very good, Giada. You're smart, beautiful, and I believe knowledgeable enough to know that I can make or break you."

She took an unsteady breath but held her ground. "Is that a threat? Surely I must be mistaken, sir. After all, we don't know one another at all."

"We're going to change that."

He pulled his arm from over her chair and then leaned back and looked at the match going on. She didn't know what to say, and then his hand slid over her knee and gave it a squeeze.

"Keeping it just business might be impossible."

She covered his hand, looked at him, and lifted it off her knee. "Then this will be the last time we ever converse because I'm not for sale."

He held her gaze, and she refused to back down, despite how scared she was.

"Watch the show, honey. We'll see," he said, getting in the last word and making her feel out of sorts.

Hell, he'd pissing her off by calling her honey in a degrading tone. She wasn't used to this kind of crap, to the bullying, the intimidation, and then threats. Who the hell was this man, and what did he want from her? What?

* * * *

Bella nudged Mateus's arm as they sat in the seat watching the pre-matches.

"What's wrong?" he asked.

She leaned closer. She swallowed hard and needed to whisper. Dominick Coglonie and his brother, cousin, and guards sat in the seats in front of them. "I got this from Giada. She needs a ride from us to Club X."

"Let me see."

She held her phone against her chest. He narrowed his eyes at her, and Major ran his hand along her thigh, giving it a squeeze. She glanced his way. All he did was raise both eyebrows at her and she knew not to argue, but Giada had been texting her, and they would see the text messages.

"Bella?" Mateus warned her.

"It's nothing. She just had planned to get there by taxi or something but now asked for a ride from us. I told her we have room in the SUV. She wants to meet by the front entryway."

He stared at her.

"Mateus, I'm not going to show you our texts back and forth."

"Why not?"

"It was a private conversation. She said things she doesn't want anyone to know, so it wouldn't be fair for you to demand to see the texts."

"Bella, is she in trouble?" Mateus asked her.

"She won't be if we meet her by the entryway, or maybe Turbo and Harley can?" she asked.

"Fuck," Mateus whispered. "This is not a good situation, her being with those men. You understand me?"

She nodded her head. "She knows that. It's why she asked for a ride."

"Tell her Harley and Turbo will escort her as she exits the room to the lobby."

Bella nodded and texted Giada back.

* * * *

"What's with all the texting?" Alajandro asked her.

"My friend's making plans about where we are meeting up."

"You said Club X. We'll drop you off, maybe come in for a drink or two."

Giada swallowed hard.

"You can do whatever you like, but I'm going with my friends. We planned it."

And then Calvarro exhaled. She thought he was going to say something, but then the match between Angelo and some big guy was getting started. Her focus went to him winning the fight, despite the obvious fact that Calvarro had bet against him. He was pretty straightforward in yelling about the Cuban guy kicking Angelo's ass. She didn't hide her smile when Angelo won, nor did she stick around to be escorted to the club. As they got up to exit, Calvarro took her arm and pulled her close.

"We'll be in touch, and when we contact you, be ready to assist. I would hate for something to happen to you on your way home one night from work. I understand that the route to your home can be a dangerous one," he threatened her then released her arm and walked away.

She turned, and Toro pulled her close. "We'll talk this week. Definitely."

He went to kiss her lips, but she turned her face, and he kissed her cheek, hard. When he pulled back, Alajandro was there, gripping her tight. He whispered in her ear.

"We don't give up easily on what we want. Remember that as you remind your guy friends that you don't date and that eventually you'll be in our bed."

He kissed her ear and cheek, and she went to pull back, but his pressed closer and kissed her lips. He ran his hand over her ass, and as she pushed his hand away from her backside, he stepped back, releasing her. She stared at them. When hands landed on her shoulders from behind, she nearly gasped, but then saw Turbo. He towered over these men.

"Are you ready, Giada?" Turbo asked.

Harley was with him looking more badass than Turbo with his beard, tattoos, and downright killer expression. She was shaking, hard.

"Ready. Thanks. Good night," she said to Alajandro and Toro, who winked.

"We'll call you and make plans," Alajandro stated with a smirk.

Turbo had his arm around her waist. He pulled her away from them and headed out. "You're okay now. You'll be safe with your friends," he said to her.

Tears filled her eyes. She sure hoped so because right now she didn't know what she'd gotten herself into.

When they arrived at the club, she and Bella headed to the ladies' room.

"What in God's name is going on?" Bella asked her as Caprice joined them.

"I don't know what is going on. It's a mess, though. I mean I should probably just head home," Giada said, and both Caprice and Bella shook their heads and crossed their arms in front of their chests.

"You've been denying your true feelings for Dominick, Andreas, and Giuseppe for too long now. It's stupid, plain and simple," Caprice stated very seriously.

She looked at them. "I don't want to go through this. I can't deal with the violence, the fear of something happening to them. I can't." She shook her head.

"Honey, do you realize that the Coglonie men are pretty powerful men but also work the sidelines. They're not in the center of danger per se like our men are. They're like the negotiators. The ice men that cool down the situations so no one gets hurt or causes trouble," Caprice added.

"I don't get it. I don't want to know. Calvarro scared me tonight, and all I was doing was showing up for two clients interested in business. That somehow tuned into more."

"They want you. Want to own you, manipulate you, and make you theirs?" Bella said to her.

"I thought so, but it seems that Calvarro wants that, too."

"What?" Caprice asked.

"Oh shit," Bella said.

"See. I don't even know what that means. Who Calvarro is or what he's involved in," Giada said to them.

Bella touched her arm and gave her a sympathetic look. "Honey, you need to get your head out of your ass and follow your heart. The Coglonies, and our men, the families, will protect you, but they can only do that if you let them and stop pushing all of us away."

"Some things are just meant to be. Before it's too late and you wind up in over your head or hurt, you need to let the men protect you," Caprice said to her.

"I don't know if I can."

"Make it simple. Whose arms do you prefer to be in? The Coglonies' or Alajandro's and Toro's?" Caprice asked.

"What?"

"It's simple. You were held by all of them, kissed by them. Hell, they each had shown possession of you with a hand on your ass. You had to feel the difference. Which did you prefer? Which ones did it for you? Which ones could you not stop thinking and fantasizing about?" Bella asked.

She looked at herself in the mirror and fixed her eyes. Bella and Caprice smiled.

"We know exactly how you feel. It's a shocker, but there's no use in fighting it. It's meant to be," Caprice said to her.

* * * *

"Where is she now?" Dominick asked Turbo once they got back downstairs to the club. They were all meeting upstairs, and he, Andreas, and Giuseppe hadn't stuck around the match long enough to see Giada leave with those other men. They were confirming that the deliveries made their way to the warehouse and were being wrapped up and shipped to the right locations. The other men were concerned for Giada's well-being but not as concerned as Dominick, Andreas, and Giuseppe.

Then Dominick found out that Giada had asked Bella for a ride. Had those men threatened her? Scared her? If so, he wanted to know.

"What is your plan of action?" Morano asked him. Mateus was there, too, and Fedarro, plus some of their main security guys.

"Things have to change, Dominick. Your brother and cousin need to protect Giada, whether she accepts that protection or not. Calvarro knows she is important to you, to us, as our woman's friend," Morano told him.

"We know that, and we'll deal with it head-on. She has no choice because we aren't giving her one," Dominick stated.

* * * *

Giada was talking to Caprice, Bella, Major, and Vito when a strong solid arm wrapped around her waist from behind. Initially she gasped, fearing who it might be, but then quickly inhaled the cologne and sensed the familiar feel of Giuseppe's arms.

"We need to talk," Giuseppe whispered into her ear.

She locked gazes with Bella, who nodded, and then Caprice, who smiled.

"Come on with me," he told her.

"Excuse us," she said to everyone standing there, and they nodded.

The men all looked serious. As Giuseppe led her through the crowds of people, he brought her to the hallway and then the elevator. He was taking her upstairs. Was it to one of the private rooms that overlooked the dance floor and club? Was it to his office? She didn't know, but it didn't really matter. Once the elevator doors closed, he caged her in against the wall. Her ass hit the mirrored wall behind her, and he loomed over her. He was the calm one out of the three Coglonies she knew.

"Did they hurt you, touch you in any way?" he asked her.

She swallowed hard. "No," she whispered.

He narrowed his eyes at her. "Don't lie to me. Never lie to any of us—ever."

She knew he was dead serious. This man was older, experienced, and a man of power and influence. Tears filled her eyes. How would she tell them that Calvarro had threatened her, hinted about wanting to see her again, and her being called upon?

He cupped her cheek as the doors opened. "This is a serious situation. It has the potential for real danger, for you to get hurt, and that just isn't fucking acceptable."

She thought he might kiss her, scold her some more, but instead, he took her hand and began to lead her from the elevator. Brew was standing there, on guard and waiting. She glanced at him, and he nodded but held a firm expression. Were they all concerned?

Giuseppe opened the door. His wavy dark-brown hair and tan complexion accentuated the bright blue tie he wore against the crisp white dress shirt. His jacket was undone, and he looked a bit frazzled. As she entered the room, all eyes fell upon her. Dominick and Andreas were there talking to Royce, Logic, and Train. They all looked her over, and Giuseppe released her hand.

"Everyone out," Dominick ordered, and she heard the tightness in his tone, the seriousness of his command, and his men walked out of the room. When the door closed, Dominick stood in front of her.

"Do you want to be with them? With Alajandro and Toro? Do you have feelings for them, an attraction?"

She had not expected that. "No." She shook her head.

His hands were on his hips, the gun and the holster in plain sight. Two buttons of his shirt were undone. He was so angry.

"Be honest. Remember what I said about lies," Giuseppe stated to her from behind her.

She looked at him. "I'm not lying. I wouldn't lie to you."

Andreas snorted as though he didn't believe her. She wondered why and looked to the right.

"I haven't lied."

"You're attracted to us. You feel it, and you claimed you didn't," he said, challenging her.

She had to decide what she wanted to do and whether taking a chance on these men was worth it. "I'm not ready to risk another broken heart."

"Give me a break," Giuseppe said, and she swallowed hard.

"Someone hurt you? An ex-lover? A boyfriend? We're not him. Cut the bullshit, Giada. Everyone has had relationships that fail, but you push us away and deny this strong attraction. Why?" Andreas pushed.

"There's more to it than that. I don't want the danger, the fear of knowing something could happen to someone I care so much for. I can't live like that. Go through that kind of sadness and pain again. I can't."

They stared at her, and tears filled her eyes.

"So hanging out with fucking Cuban mob bosses who have slit throats for minor insults is less dangerous than being with fucking us?" Dominick raised his voice.

"I didn't know he was a Cuban mob boss."

Dominick stepped closer, and she didn't move. Couldn't move. He towered over her, and through his blue dress shirt, she could see his bulging muscles. He, too, wore his gun and holster and no longer had the jacket on covering it. His hands were on his hips.

"Calvarro Torres is a very, very bad man, Giada—the kind of man who will own you without you even realizing it, and when and if you do realize he owns you, it's too late."

She swallowed hard, could see how pissed off he was. She shivered. "He doesn't own me," she whispered, and her voice cracked.

"He wants you," Giuseppe said, pressing up against her back.

Her lips parted as he held on to her shoulders, and Dominick gripped her hips. He lowered to look her in the eyes.

"He can't have you," Dominick said through clenched teeth.

She stared up into his dark brown eyes, looked at his firm lips, that distinguished nose, and serious expression. "I don't even know what happened. I don't," she whispered as tears filled her eyes.

"You'll explain it to us so we understand. We'll protect you." He eased his hand to her cheek and used his thumb to stroke her lower lip.

He stared at her, and the feel of Dominick's finger stroking her lip, the intense look in his eyes, made her think of Bella's and

Caprice's words to her, about how it felt when the men touched her and who she was attracted to.

"You need protecting, baby. You're a beautiful, tiny young thing. My God, I don't want to think about it."

He stared at her lips, gripped her jaw, and then lowered his mouth to hers and kissed her.

Giuseppe released her shoulders, and Dominick wrapped her up in his arms. She felt lost in his embrace. She kissed him back, allowed him full access to her mouth, but when his palm slid along her ass, the size large enough to cover most of her ass cheek, his larger size intimidated her. She tightened up, and he eased his mouth from hers.

"What's wrong?"

She shook her head.

He gave her a little shake and tilted his head at her. "Honesty, no lies."

She swallowed. "You're so big and filled with muscles. I'm lost in your embrace. It's intimidating."

He narrowed his eyes at her and looked over her breasts then to her lips as he wrapped her up tight. "You're protected in this embrace. Cared for and cherished. Now give your men some loving. They've been more than patient these last few months, never mind having to watch other men touch you, kiss you, knowing that those men want you in their beds when you're our woman." He slowly released her to Giuseppe.

Giuseppe reached for her hips but didn't pull her close. He stared down at her lips and let his palm slide along her hip and lower back. He waited for her to initiate the kiss. How couldn't she? The man was gorgeous. She stepped closer to him and stood up on tiptoes in her heels. His arm tightened around her waist, and Giuseppe's palm grazed her ass as he lowered his mouth to meet hers. When their lips touched, sparks flew, that connection intensified, and she was lost in the man's control and embrace. Giuseppe plunged his tongue in deeply then ran his palm along her ass and one up to cup her breast. She pulled back.

"Giuseppe," she whispered and lowered her eyes. She stepped back, only for him to pull her close by her ass and thrust against her.

He squinted at her. "You're going to be our woman. No other men but the three of us," he said to her so seriously.

These men were experienced. Just the way they held her, touched her, showed that experience. He tapped her ass.

"Andreas's turn to feel this sexy body and taste those delicious lips."

She turned toward Andreas. His expression was hard. He was the quietest, the most serious and lethal. The man she felt and assumed did all the rough stuff. He was retired military, Special Forces. She gulped as tears stung her eyes. Could she let down her guard, forget about the past and about Jimmy to let Andreas in, too?

He took her hand and looked down at it. He placed it into his and stared at the difference in size. Then he slid his other hand up her wrist to her shoulder and then under her hair. He gripped the locks possessively and tilted her head up toward him. Her lips parted as she held his gaze, feeling a mix of concern and desire for more.

"This is it, Giada. We're taking a chance on you, too, on this."

He then lowered down, she thought to kiss her mouth, but instead, he inhaled against her neck and trailed his lips softly against the skin as his grip on her tightened.

She anticipated his lips touching hers, and she wanted him to kiss her, wanted to feel his lips possess hers as Dominick's and Giuseppe's had only moments ago. It was crazy, wild, and then he trailed his mouth along her jaw to the corner of her mouth and kissed her. Andreas took his time, kissed her tenderly then more fully. When his hand started to slide up under her dress as she moaned into his mouth, she knew she needed to slow things down. She gripped his shoulder and pressed her hand against the hand trying to move under her dress.

His fingers were over her ass, the tips sliding in the crack. She felt her pussy react, and she gripped him tight.

"Andreas, I need slow. There are things to explain so you understand."

He narrowed his eyes at her. "You're still holding back. You're unsure. Why, when this is so damn powerful?"

"It's what holds me back. What gives me the fear to not open my heart, to not date or get close to a man, to any man."

"Who was this guy, and what the hell did he do?" Dominick asked, sounding angry again.

She pulled back from Andreas, instantly feeling the loss of his hands on her body. She wiped her eyes before a tear fell. "His name was Jimmy. He was Special Forces. We dated for three years, were going to get married and start a family, but he died in combat."

"Damn, Giada," Giuseppe whispered.

"A Special Forces soldier?" Andreas asked her, and she stared up at him and nodded.

"I've been too scared to date any man."

"When did he pass?" Dominick asked.

"Two years ago."

"You haven't been with a man since him?" Giuseppe asked.

"He was my only lover ever."

The expression on Andreas's face was indescribable. She didn't know what he would say or do, and when he shook his head and then reached out, grabbed a fistful of the material of her dress, and pulled her into his arms and hugging her tight, she was shocked. The tears fell, and she hugged him back.

"You're so damn special, Giada. Guys come back and they have no one, or they change so much that they're not even the same person. I couldn't imagine having to leave you to serve and then praying that you would be there for me when I returned. You're a damn angel, Giada. Your Jimmy would want you to be happy, not lonely. A soldier wants those he cares about to be safe and to be happy. We can do that, Giada. You can do that for us, too."

* * * *

Andreas took her hand and brought her over to the couch. He sat down, and she took the seat next to him, crossed her legs, and then looked at Dominick and Giuseppe. His cousins pulled over two chairs and placed them in front of the couch and Giada.

"Let's go through this situation so we know where things stand. Then we can go downstairs and enjoy the rest of the night with family and friends and celebrate Angelo's win," Dominick said to her.

Andreas looked at Giada as she answered their questions. He'd felt protective of her from day one, and that protectiveness and desire had turned to a possessiveness that just seemed to get stronger. From the moment she'd been nearly abducted, he'd felt compelled to be her protector. Thank God he had been in the hospital room that day she was going to be discharged, or she wouldn't be here right now. He squeezed her hand and put it on his thigh. She talked about her job, about the business she was doing with Alajandro and Toro, and about meeting up with their cousin Calvarro.

Andreas knew Calvarro's ways of handling things. He was dirty, he was gruesome, and he would surely go after Giada. Andreas saw how Calvarro looked at her, kept her close, whispered into her ear, and put that fear on her face.

"You're not to go see them again. No meetings with Calvarro. Doesn't matter if he makes a demand. Your response is that he needs to make that appointment through me," Dominick stated firmly.

Andreas clenched his teeth. This could get bad.

"I don't understand. How would that work?" she asked Dominick.

He leaned closer, placed his hands on her knees, and squeezed. "He'll know immediately that you're our woman. That he can't touch you, pursue you, or make a move."

"Unless he's fucking stupid and ready to start a war," Giuseppe stated very seriously.

"I wouldn't put it past the narcissistic bastard. He thinks who the fuck he is," Andreas stated.

Dominick stared at Giada. "I understand your fears and why you pushed us away. We do have dangerous jobs, and we are engaged in activities that you do not need to know about. But you need to be aware that we have enemies. However, in you avoiding this attraction, you inadvertently put yourself right next to a man, and men, that could destroy your life. You ran from us. Don't make that same mistake again. Let us protect you, Giada. Let us see where this attraction leads us."

"I need slow, Dominick. I need to recondition my mind, my senses, to things."

"Understandable, but there's no holding back. Talk to us about them, about your concerns and fears, and in private. When we walk out that door tonight and go down there to the club, you go as our woman. And we go as your men. Understood?" Dominick asked her firmly.

She looked at him, licked her lower lip, and looked at Andreas and Giuseppe. "Yes, I understand."

Dominick stood, reached out his hands for her to take, and lifted her up and into his arms. He wrapped her up tight, as his cousin's arms encased her as if she was precious. "Before we go down, one more kiss to hold me off until later tonight." He then kissed her lips and ran his palm along her ass and her back before he released her. "You need to fix up?"

She nodded, but then Andreas pulled her close and kissed her. He felt her curves and imagined what she looked like naked. Giuseppe cleared his throat, and then Andreas released her to him. He kissed her and then led her toward the table where her small purse was.

Andreas looked at Dominick as Dominick texted the guys. A knock sounded on the door as Giada finished fixing her lip gloss. She ran her hands along her dress. Andreas held out his hand.

"Let's go enjoy the night with family and friends."

She took his hand, and the four of them, plus Royce and Logic, headed out of the office and into the elevator to the club. Andreas felt uptight and anxious. Would Giada come home with them tonight and let them truly into her heart, or would she need more time, a sense of control and separation? He didn't want to leave her alone, accessible to an attack. She wouldn't be allowed to go home alone tonight. He saw how Calvarro and the other two men looked at her with desire, lust in their eyes. They wanted his woman, and that was never going to happen.

* * * *

"So, can we assume the conversation went well upstairs, and you're accepting Andreas, Dominick, and Giuseppe as your protectors and men?" Bella asked Giada. She stood by the bar with Caprice, Bella, Alessa, Alda, Donata, and Fina.

"I'm accepting them, but I'm still not ready to be intimate." She glanced their way. The men were watching her closely.

"Well, that won't be a problem for long. Believe me, once you get tag-teamed, it's pretty damn hard to say no when it feels so right," Caprice said.

Bella chuckled. "Isn't that the truth?"

"We wouldn't know. None of us have engaged in any ménages, although I have to say that Turbo, Covan, Jack, and Harley are definitely men I would like to make my first ménage encounter with," Donata stated, looking toward Turbo and the guys.

Alessa gave her arm a slap. "You are so full of crap. You were just saying how intimidating all the security guys are. You talk a great game, Donata, but come down to it, and no way anything is happening."

The others laughed.

"Yeah, besides, you can't take like all four hot guys for yourself. You need to share," Alda added.

"Well, I think that Royce, Logic, Train, and Brew are pretty hot, but that doesn't mean they would want to share the same woman. Hell, I would pass out if one of them flirted with me, never mind wanted to go out with me," Alda stated.

"How do you know any of the security guys are even into that whole ménage thing?" Fina asked.

"Who do you have your eyes on?" Bella asked Fina.

Giada couldn't help but smirk. She knew who Fina had eyes for.

Fina got all quiet. "No one. I'm playing it safe for a while."

"Playing it safe? What do you mean?" Caprice asked her.

"She was hanging out a few weeks back when all the crazy stuff was going on with Rayanna and Giada, and she met these two guys and started hanging out with them," Donata said.

"Donata, don't. It isn't a big deal, and it's over with. They aren't calling or texting anymore," Fina stated.

"Wait. Some guys were bothering you, and you didn't tell any of us or our men?" Caprice asked.

"It was handled," Fina stated.

"By who?" Giada asked, feeling concerned.

Donata chuckled. "Tell them or I will."

"One of Dmitri's guys," Fina looked away from them.

Giada was shocked, and so was everyone but Donata. They started whistling and teasing her. Poor Fina was as red as a cherry.

"Oh God, the Russian mob. Look at you, Fina. Part-time events coordinator and stock trader. All prim and proper, following the straight and narrow," Caprice teased.

"I wouldn't go that far. She was pretty entertaining in the Dominican Republic, as we all recall," Alessa said, and they laughed.

"Oh yeah, Mario and Johnny were their names. They worked for Mateus or something at one of the security firms in Miami," Alda stated.

"Interesting," Bella said.

"Cut it out. I just fooled around with them, and it wasn't anything more than a good time on vacation." Fina slid her hand along her hips in the tight skirt she wore.

"Rayanna, Dmitri, and the crew are supposed to be coming to town to visit soon. Are you going to talk to your friend, or was it friends?" Caprice asked.

"Nothing happened between them and me."

"Them? Which ones?" Bella asked.

"Oh brother. Thanks a bunch, Donata. I'll remember this." Fina drank the rest of her girlie fruit drink and then moved past them to place it on the bar.

Giada smiled. "I love you guys. I never would have made it through the heartache over Jimmy, my uncle Les being a jerk, or anything in life without you guys."

"Aw, we love you, too, Giada." Bella hugged her shoulder.

"How is Uncle Les? Have you had to bail him out of jail or anything?" Donata asked.

"Donata," Caprice scolded.

Giada chuckled. "No, I haven't. It's been fine. I really don't talk to him, and after I had to go pick him up at some shit bar a couple of weeks ago at three o'clock in the morning, I think I'm done with him."

They all responded with shock and concern.

"You can't do that kind of stuff. Now that you're with the Coglonie men, you need to make them aware of Uncle Les if he calls or asks for help," Bella told her.

"I guess I'm going to need to learn a lot. My big concern is for my job. I don't know how I'm going to see Alajandro and Toro again for work and how to handle it."

"Oh, don't worry about that. I'm sure Dominick has already sent out the message that you belong to him, his brother, and their cousin. Those men would be asking for trouble if they contacted you anyway," Bella told her.

"If they do, tell your men right away. No messing around, Giada. Those are guys with connections to the Cuban mafia. That's heavy shit," Aldo told her, and they all agreed.

Giada felt her belly ache, and she placed her hand over it, looked past the girls, and locked gazes with Andreas. He squinted, and she gave a soft smile and listened to her friends talk some more. She didn't know what she was going to do tonight. When she thought about sleeping with them, her heart ached, and she felt guilty. She needed to get rid of these feeling that stood in the way of what she wanted. Dominick, Andreas, and Giuseppe. She had to.

* * * *

"So what did you find out?" Mateus asked Dominick as they stood near the bar watching Bella, Caprice, Giada, and their friends talking.

"Enough to know that Calvarro and his two cousins want our Giada. Considering the current business dealings we're involved in, I'd say he had bad intentions."

"Dominick, what is she going to do about work and dealing with these men? She can't not do that or quit that job," Mateus asked.

"Why the fuck not?" Giuseppe asked and took a sip of his brandy.

Mateus chuckled, and so did Sunny, who stood next to Giuseppe.

"Seriously, the woman is a workaholic. Bella said she doesn't date ever," Mateus told them.

"We know. Turns out the reason she was holding back was because of an old boyfriend. A soldier who she'd planned to marry died in combat," Dominick told them. Sunny whistled low.

"Is that why Andreas is in a dead stare at her right now?" Sunny asked.

"I'm sure that hit home for him. He survived when a lot of his friends didn't," Giuseppe stated.

"Could be a good thing she's the one you set your eyes on. She might be good for Andreas. Maybe make him a little less hostile," Mateus teased, and they snickered.

"Never happen," Sunny said.

Dominick noticed that Andreas was staring at his cell phone and looked pissed off. Dominick caught his eyes, and Andreas walked over toward them.

"What's wrong?" Mateus asked.

"They're watching her fucking apartment building. Brew just texted now."

"Shit," Sunny said.

"What are you going to do?" Major asked.

"Going caveman isn't going to work on a woman like Giada. Could scare the hell out of her," Mateus said to them in warning.

"She won't go home without security from now on. We promised to take things slow because of this guy she lost and cared about. That doesn't mean we can't stay nearby and protect her. We'll figure it out." Dominick locked gazes with Andreas, who didn't look happy at all.

* * * *

Giada gasped as Dominick clasped her wrists behind her back with one hand while cupping her cheek and head, kissing her. She moaned into his mouth. The man was dominant, controlling, and in a way that totally aroused her. She found herself pressing against him, reciprocating the kiss until his hand slid from her cheek to her breast.

She shivered as her mind processed what was happening here. She wanted them—wanted to be with them, trust them, continue to feel how protected she was with them—but she wasn't ready to be intimate. Would this drive them mad? Would it make them annoyed with her? They were older, more experienced men, and she wasn't stupid. These men could have any woman they wanted in their beds. They could have sex every night if they wanted to. Why did that aggravate her and make her jealous? She pulled back, only for him to release her lips and catch his breath, his hold on her wrists still firm. He gripped her jaw and stared at her with dark, serious eyes.

"I want you in our bed, in our arms, where I know you're safe and all ours. I don't want you to fucking go home," he whispered through clenched teeth.

Tears stung her eyes. She parted her lips. "I'm trying. I'm…I'm just not like other women you guys are used to. I can't pretend to be someone I'm not. To look at sleeping with you as just meaningless sex."

The hands landed on her shoulder.

"Meaningless? Definitely not meaningless." Giuseppe joined the conversation.

She knew that he and Andreas had stood right there watching Dominick kiss her, touch her, and try to convince her to go home with them instead of going home alone.

Giuseppe caressed her hair and then cupped her head, softly tilting her head up toward him. He lowered. "Definitely not meaningless." He kissed her.

Dominick released her wrists, and she turned into Giuseppe's kiss and ran her hands up his chest under his dress jacket and to his shoulders. She felt his palm slide along her ass and squeeze her against him hard. She felt his thick erection, and she wished she could let the walls down and take this chance. If she went home with them, had sex with them, what if things didn't work out? What if it went wrong? Then she would have made a huge mistake and wind up with a broken heart because she'd given her all and they saw it as sexual pleasure, control, dominance, and possession.

Giuseppe released her lips and kissed her chin. "You're killing us leaving us like this," he said against her cheek.

She held his gaze. "Don't be angry with me. Please understand I've made love with only one man. That's one man ever, and you three..." She shook her head. "You three have been with who knows how many women."

Giuseppe wrapped her in his arms tighter, nearly taking her breath away. He stared down into her eyes, and she held onto his shoulders.

"None of that matters—not the past, not any other lovers for any of us. What matters is now, Giada, what we feel and how powerful this connection is. We want every bit of you. We want to explore this body, learn what turns you on, what makes you beg for more cock."

"Oh God," she said on an exhale.

"I think you're scaring her." Dominick chuckled.

Giuseppe held her gaze. "No, I'm not scaring her. She wants it, too, but she's still holding up that wall, and we need to break it down and show her how perfect this will be." He kissed her again, lowered her feet to the floor, and slowly released her. "Andreas will take you home with Train and Logic." He tapped her ass as she looked at Andreas.

When she went to grab her purse, Dominick took her hand and stopped her. That dark, serious expression and those brown eyes held hers steady.

"Don't be scared when you see the extra security around. Brew will be there when you two get to the apartment. One guy will remain downstairs with Donny and another outside your apartment door."

"What? Why? Is that necessary?"

Dominick reached up and stroked her cheek. "They're watching your apartment."

"Who?" she asked, heart pounding.

"Men working for Calvarro."

Her eyes widened, and she looked at Andreas, who had his arms crossed and appeared pissed off. Then she looked at Giuseppe, whose lips were in a thin line, and he was obviously angry, too. She could have sworn she heard him grinding his teeth. She suddenly wasn't sure about going home, but she couldn't flip-flop. She had a life to live, and she hadn't done anything wrong to merit Calvarro and his men watching her apartment.

"Then I guess it will be good to head home and have them see that Andreas is with me. They'll know you're protecting me."

"They'll know soon enough that you're our woman, just as soon as you stay with us and we stay with you."

She gulped. "So this is a means to show some sort of ownership to protect me from harm? That's why you wanted me to stay the night with you? To have sex with you?" She felt insulted and emotional.

"I'm not even going to respond to that. Don't minimize what is happening here. You're already getting away with going home alone without one of us staying the night in your bed with you. These walls you have up will be coming down. The sooner, the better," Dominick stated firmly.

Now she felt guilty and bad for insulting him, them, and what was happening. The hang-up was with her. She needed to process her emotions and desires. She needed to be sure that this was right and that it was time to let go, let the walls down, and allow them into her heart. Well, they were already in her heart, and she cared for them, even worried about what harm could come to them if this Cuban-gang thing got out of hand. She exhaled and felt jittery and nervous as Andreas escorted her out of the office in the club and down to the waiting SUV.

Was this going to be a new way of life for her, like it was for Bella, Caprice, Gisella, Rayanna, and Adelina? Maybe she needed to talk to them a bit more? As they drove to her apartment, she found comfort in having a man as big and capable as Andreas with her. She tried not to read into the fact that he was a soldier like Jimmy had been. She wouldn't compare. There was no comparison. As capable as Jimmy had been as a man and a soldier, Andreas was so much more. He was hard and fierce, not as talkative as his cousins. She absorbed everything about him. His hard, thick thighs and how they looked in the dress pants he wore. The way the suit clung to his wide, thick shoulders and muscular arms. He had a hand on her knee the moment she crossed her legs, and it sent warmth and desire right to her cunt. She readjusted her position in the seat multiple times.

When they got to her apartment, sure enough Brew was outside waiting by the door to greet them.

"You're not staying the night?" he asked Andreas in a tone that made her feel worse.

Everyone seemed to want to accept this joining and relationship but her and the damn hang-ups.

"Not tonight," he replied in a sharp tone.

As they walked into the lobby, she locked onto Donny standing there with one guy she recognized as one of the Coglonie security men.

"You went over everything with them?" Andreas asked Brew, who accompanied them up into the elevator.

"Yes." Brew hit the button for her floor.

When the doors opened, she felt as if her legs were going to give out she was so nervous and affected by all this stuff. Her life had already changed, and she hadn't even had sex with the Coglonie men. The second set of doors opened, and she saw another man was right outside her door.

"Mike, keep in contact with Toby downstairs," Andreas stated.

"Got it, sir."

"We'll inform you of the morning schedule when I come out," Andreas told them.

Brew nodded.

She handed over her keys to the apartment, and Andreas opened the door. She went inside feeling his hand at her hips. He closed the door and looked around the place. She placed her purse on the coffee table and turned to look at him.

Andreas stared at her. His eyes swept over her, and every part of her came alive again. How did these men do this to her? Three men. She was going to belong—no, she belonged—to three made men.

He licked his lower lip and closed the space between them. He stared at her eyes, her lips as she gripped his arms and held onto him.

"I know you feel it. You couldn't sit still because your body aches for us. It aches to be claimed by us."

He lowered down and kissed her. She kissed him back and relished the feel of his hands sliding up and down her ass and thighs and how his big, strong arms pulled her tight against his rock-solid muscles. She felt the gun against her hip, and her pussy wept.

He released her lips and backstepped her toward the couch.

"I need more, Giada, something more to get me through the night. To help me tamp down my need to fuck and claim every damn fucking inch of you. I want to bury my cock so deep inside of you that you cry out for mercy." He sucked on her neck as he unzipped her dress.

"Andreas. Oh God." She exhaled as he lowered her to the couch, half lying over her as he stared into her eyes. She gripped his shoulders, could feel how loose her dress was on top. It was strapless. One push down and he would see her breasts, maybe suck her nipples and make her wetter than she already was. Did she want that?

"A little more. Just a little more."

He eased his long, thick finger along the trim of her top then gently pushed down. Her breast emerged, and he squinted. She could see the veins by his temples pulsate. He licked his lips.

"Incredible."

He lowered his mouth. She watched as his lips parted, and he licked the tip and began to feast. "Oh, Andreas." She tilted her hips upward, and he sucked harder, slid a hand up under her dress against her thigh, and squeezed her hip. He lifted his hip and was going to slide between her legs when she gripped his shoulders. "Stop. It's too much. Giuseppe and Dominick aren't here."

"They can be here in a flash, baby. One fucking call."

He was so harsh, firm in his tone that it made her heart race and her pussy spasm. She was out of her mind pushing him away. He lowered his mouth to her other breast. She ran her fingers through his hair. She squinted her eyes and wanted to let go. She did, and now she felt stupid for pushing Dominick and Giuseppe away. She was going to miss the three of them tonight. She was going to regret this.

"Please, Andreas."

He lifted his mouth from her breast then cupped it. "You're more than a handful. I want to strip you naked, see what's going to be ours."

She shook her head. "I'm not ready for that."

He stared at her as if he were trying to read her mind. He lifted off of and offered a hand. She placed a hand into his and used the other to hold up her dress. When she stood with his assistance, she kept a hand against her top.

"Walk me to the door," he said to her.

She did. When they got there, he swallowed hard.

"We'll make plans for tomorrow."

"I have to teach a martial arts class in the morning at the dojo and then stop somewhere to run an errand."

"You teach martial arts?" he asked.

"Kids' classes."

"We all need to talk and to get to know one another," he said to her.

"Exactly," she whispered, and it was as though he understood her reservations about jumping into bed with them.

He brought her hand to his lips and kissed the top, and then he pressed a kiss to her forehead. "Tomorrow." He released her hand and turned to open the door. "Lock this up," he ordered.

She gulped and nodded.

When the door closed, she locked the locks and then looked toward the couch. She already regretted not staying with the men. Then she thought of Jimmy. It was going to be a long, sleepless night.

Chapter 7

"What do you need from me? I've done everything so far that you asked. You made promises, too," Les said to the man over the phone.

"Be patient and be ready when the call comes in to do your part."

"You should move quickly. The Coglonie men are pushing her to be their woman. I heard that she was with them last night and that one of them, Andreas, took her home. They have security there protecting her."

"We know this."

"Well then, how can you get her out of this situation like you promised? How? They'll ruin her life, and she deserves better."

"The boss knows what he's doing. It will all work out. Just keep the phone nearby and be ready to do what is asked of you."

"How about the money, the promises made to me for helping? Giada is going to fight this. She doesn't realize what those Coglonie men are capable of. I don't want her hurt. That's what this is all about."

"She won't get hurt if you do your part. You know the money is to benefit you, as well. It will work out. Be ready."

Les closed up the phone and then paced his small, dirty place. He was living in filth, barely surviving. If this situation didn't go through soon, he would wind up on the streets, in the shelters, or begging Giada for help. She needed him to get her out of this bad situation. Those men he was helping knew what the Coglonies, the Fiorres, and Costanzas were capable of. Giada hadn't a clue. This was best for her, even if she fought it and was too stupid to realize the men didn't love her. They just wanted to own her. He would be ready. Her destiny lay in another man's arms, not in the Coglonies' arms.

* * * *

"Where is she now?" Dominick asked Andreas.

"Brew said she's showering and changing and then needs to run an errand," Andreas told him.

"An errand? Where?" Giuseppe asked.

"Brooklyn," Andreas said.

"Brooklyn? What's in Brooklyn?" Dominick asked him.

"I don't know. She tried telling him she needed to go alone, but Brew said it wasn't happening. What do you want to do?" Andreas asked.

Dominick exhaled. "I don't like it. After last night and what happened between us, between you and her, Andreas, I would think she would want to get here and be with us. Maybe she really doesn't have the same feelings."

"I wouldn't say that. Whatever she needs to do, she insisted that she needed to do it first before meeting us."

"Have Brew keep us informed where she's going as soon as he has an address," Dominick stated.

Andreas's phone buzzed. He glanced down, squinted, and exhaled. "I'm going to go there."

"Where?" Giuseppe asked.

Andreas showed him his cell phone and the text message from Brew.

"Cypress Hills National Cemetery?" Giuseppe read out the words.

"It's a military cemetery. She's going to visit Jimmy." Andreas headed out of the room.

Dominick looked at Giuseppe. "I've never seen Andreas like this. To know that Giada had been in love with a soldier who had died in combat has got to have crazy shit going through Andreas's head. Now this."

Giuseppe exhaled. "You know as well as I do that Andreas hasn't been the same man since he left the service. He survived, and his friends didn't. Men he knew for years, men who had families. He understands what she's going through. I think it's part of why this relationship is going to work so well."

"It's only going to work if Andreas and Giada are willing to take the chance, put the past behind them, and let go."

"I think he's already letting go. He's talked more the last couple weeks than he has in years. This could be what Giada needs, going to the gravesite. Maybe getting some emotions out. She has protection with her, and Andreas will be minutes behind them. Let's just see what happens," Giuseppe said.

Dominick's cell phone rang, and he saw it was Mateus. "Hey, Mateus, what's going on?"

"We have a problem."

"What is that?"

"One of the trucks with two guys Sunny hired to do a delivery of merchandise somehow wound up being delivered to one of Calvarro's warehouses instead."

"What?"

"Not a fucking mix-up. Calvarro must have gotten wind of the deliveries and had his guys redirect the route. It's stolen shit. How do you want to handle this?" Mateus asked.

"Head-on. The fucker is challenging all of us. He wants to make this first move to giving us trouble, then he'll regret it."

"I wonder if this has something to do with a sexy, blue-eyed woman the three of you Coglonies have yet to claim," Mateus said.

"We're all in this together. Let's call for a meeting and see how we want to handle it."

"Plan on taking that shipment back?" Mateus asked.

"How about we plan on taking something of theirs to show Calvarro who has more connections and power in this city?"

"Exactly. I'll work on it with Sunny and the others. We'll be in touch later today."

"Is he just being sore about our takeover, or is it he's pissed about Giada and not getting her in his bed?" Giuseppe asked.

"Probably both and then some. You saw him last night. He wants her."

"Well, he can't have her. She's ours."

"Not yet she isn't. You know as well as I do if she doesn't fully accept us, our protection, being our woman, that it will be more difficult to protect her. We still need to resolve this work issue and how she's supposed to deal with these men. We can't ask her to quit her job," Dominick stated.

"Why the fuck not? We can take care of her, no problem," Giuseppe said, and Dominick gave him a funny look.

"I hear what you're saying, but the reality is that she's an independent, professional woman who has made a career in the finance and banking world. We can't force her to leave all that hard work behind. What we can do is ensure she is never left alone with Alajandro, Toro, or Calvarro. That, we have control over."

* * * *

"It all went according to plan. That was the largest shipment, too, over a hundred grand of product," Loppo said to Calvarro.

"Good. Maybe that will send the message that they can't push us around without us pushing back. I mean what the fuck is this shit? The Costanzas, Sanclare, the Fiorres, and even the Coglonies, who hardly ever dabble in this shit, are all moving in on our territory and our products, imported from our country, not made here in the States. This is bullshit," Calvarro stated.

"What is the next step?" Loppo asked.

"We ensure that we keep Giada close and that she is accessible to Alajandro and Toro, and, of course, that means to me. That way, when we plan negotiations to maintain dominance in this market over all others, we have some cards to play with."

"So if you don't like what these men offer when you ask for a sit-down, then you're going after the woman?"

"Exactly. Obviously since the Coglonies provided security for her last night and this morning, she is important to them."

"You were interested in her, too," Loppo stated.

"What man wouldn't be? You saw her. Plus, Alajandro and Toro really want her, too. Anything can happen. She could be the playing tool we need to negotiate our terms. We shall see. We play nice from here on out unless provoked not to. Patience is key here, Loppo. Patience."

* * * *

"Can you wait here please, Brew? I need some time alone."

He nodded and watched her walk along the long paved pathway of the cemetery. His chest tightened. He'd overheard the bosses and knew that Giada hadn't stayed with them last night because of this man she lost, a soldier who she was in love with but who'd died in combat. It was sad to learn of her loss, and in the weeks they had all spent around her when protecting her, they all saw a side to their bosses they had never seen. Dominick, Andreas, and Giuseppe were in love with Giada. She was special. That was for sure. Each of the security guys thought so, and they were pleased for their bosses. Brew was concerned, though. The men she had been doing business with were bad men, men capable of terrible, violent acts to get what they wanted. He took her protection seriously, and he wasn't surprised when the other SUV pulled up, and instead, of it being extra security and Train, Andreas stepped out of the back seat.

* * * *

Giada made her way down the path and to the perfect little spot by the bench and tree. Jimmy Lawrence's gravesite. She read the military dedication on the headstone, showing years of sacrifice and his birth and death dates, along with an American flag. She pulled the old flag from its spot and replaced it with a new, bright-colored American flag. Her soldier, her lover, and her best friend now gone forever.

She pressed her hand to the grave. Instantly tears stung her eyes, and her chest tightened. She felt different today, her heart heavy with emotion yet determination to get through this and make the necessary changes she needed to. For the past two years, she'd come here often. At first, it was every day, sometimes more than once, or otherwise for hours. Rain, snow, wind, or sunshine, she sat here and sobbed, remembering the good times as well as the bad. She'd asked God why he'd been taken from her and asked God for strength to go on living.

She closed her eyes, kept her hand on the tombstone, and saw Jimmy's bright smile; his firm, muscular jaw; and that dimple in his right cheek she always brought out in him when he smiled wide. His image was a little fuzzy in her head. Was she forgetting what he looked like?

Tears filled her eyes. It had been months since she'd come here. Not out of forgetting or not caring but out of confusion as to what she was feeling for the Coglonie men. She knew she would never forget Jimmy. He would always have a part of her heart. She would talk about him, remembering their love and their laughter. Last night while she lay in bed unable to sleep, she'd thought of Jimmy, and she'd thought of Andreas, Dominick, and Giuseppe.

She analyzed her feelings for the three men and what she found so appealing about each of them. She kept coming back to the same things. They each made her feel protected. They each had a way of caring for her and showing their desires. Those expressions in their eyes and the intensity of this powerful connection between the four of them could not be ignored any longer. She'd realized last night that truly the only thing standing in her way of accepting them as her men, her lovers, was Jimmy. Jimmy was no longer here. Jimmy would want her to be happy, and he would want her safe. She wasn't safe without the Coglonie men around her, not just because of men like Calvarro but also because that was how the Coglonie men made her feel—safe, secure, loved. Hell, she was fighting being in love with them. Why?

It was time—time to move on, time to use her heart to love another man, in this case, three men, three men she honestly already loved and felt stupid admitting that. Tears filled her eyes.

"Oh, Jimmy, I'll never forget you, baby. I'll never ever forget you." The tears fell, blocking her vision a moment as her heart ached. She could remember his kisses, his strong embrace, the way he completed her. She could remember the instant loss each time he left for another tour of duty and the ultimate emptiness that she'd felt learning that he was dead, that he would never come through that door again smiling, ready to make love to her because he'd missed her terribly.

She sniffled and then gulped. "It's time to move on. I guess I came here today looking for your blessing in some way or maybe just to give you the respect I feel you deserve being the only man I ever loved, until now."

She wiped her eyes and exhaled. She chuckled. "I love them, and I haven't even been with them, haven't gone on dates, haven't made love to them, yet I love them already, and I'm scared Jimmy. I'm scared of losing them, of not getting enough time to love them fully. I mean I know that's crazy, Jimmy. I know it, but I can't help it.

"When I lost you, a part of me died. My friends tell me it's time to love again, to give my heart, and to not to be alone and afraid anymore. I believe that Andreas, Dominick, and Giuseppe are the ones for me, that they'll protect me and love me the way you would want them to, the way I so desperately need them to.

"It's so crazy. Maybe I'm wrong. Maybe I'm just tired of being alone. Maybe I just think I love them, even though they can't possibly love me, not yet, but that's a risk I'm ready to take. I have to take it. I can't stand being without them, and pushing them away is stupid. I only pushed them away because of guilt, and that isn't fair. I don't want to be alone anymore, fighting these feelings. I hope you're okay with this, Jimmy. I'll never forget you. I'll never stop loving you, but I need these men. I want them in my life, in my heart, and to be part of them. I do."

The tears rolled down her cheeks, and she sniffled. Her vision blurred once again. She felt the presence behind her, but before she could turn, strong arms wrapped around her midsection and held her tight.

Andreas. She tightened up but then exhaled. Had he heard all she said?

His lips pressed against her neck by her ear. "I'm going to take such good care of you, baby. My cousins and I adore you so much already. I know this is hard. I understand it, Giada. I do. Jimmy won't need to worry about you anymore. I'm taking over his job, his role as protector from here on out. You're mine to love, to hold, and to cherish. I'm not taking his place. The three of us aren't. We're starting a new journey—together."

He squeezed her tighter and continued kissing her neck and then held her as she let the tears fall, letting go of the past and preparing herself to take the leap of faith into the future, a future with Andreas, Dominick, and Giuseppe Coglonie—three made men.

* * * *

"Where are we headed?" Andreas asked Giada. She sat in the back of the SUV with him, leaning on his shoulder and holding onto his arm.

"Wherever Dominick and Giuseppe are," she whispered.

He looked toward the front seat where Train was driving and Logic was in the passenger seat.

"They're at the penthouse," Train told him.

Andreas nodded. He kept his hand on Giada's knee and stroked her thigh.

She held his hand when they exited the SUV in the underground garage. There were multiple men from the security team there as a precaution. They all said hello to Giada, who said hello back. Andreas had a feeling that all their security team liked her. They would protect her like they protected him and his cousins, too. She stared straight ahead once they were in the private elevator. Train and Logic stood in front of them and Giada behind them and in front of Andreas. He placed his hands on her hips. The blue sweater she wore hung off her shoulders, revealing some fancy blue lace halter-type tank that matched the sweater. His hands looked so huge on her hips. He loved how the swell of her ass stuck out in the dark black pants she wore, dramatized by the low-heeled black boots giving her a little height but not much compared to him and the two men in front of her. She eased back against him and placed her hand over his. She stroked his fingers there. The anticipation of what was coming today had his heart racing as well as filled with apprehension.

He knew that he wasn't a great man, that he had done shit in his life to survive and even just to deal with the nightmares in his head and release the tension the military life caused in him. He'd fucked up a lot of people in a fit of rage, but none of them were good people. They were criminals, killers, men who did damage to the weak and preyed on them. Transitioning to organized crime had not been so difficult.

The doors opened, Train pressed in the pass code, and the short entryway appeared. "We'll be around if you need us," Train said to him.

Andreas nodded.

Logic gave Giada a smile. "Glad to see you here where you're safest." He then headed down the hallway.

Train remained, and as Andreas pulled Giada along with him to the next set of doors, he saw Train's security replacement coming their way.

As they entered the penthouse, Giada stopped short. "Holy God, this is amazing," she whispered.

He brought her deeper into the room, the heels of her ankle boots clicking on the marble flooring, showing her the view high up and over the city. She held onto his arm and walked with him toward the window, and then she wrapped her arm around his waist and leaned into him.

"You like it?"

"What's not to like, Andreas? This is an amazing home."

He inhaled the scent of her shampoo and caressed her back. He felt happy that she was here with him.

"Giada."

She heard her name, and Andreas released her to Giuseppe. He and Dominick were standing there, dressed casually in T-shirts and jeans. They stared at her, and she didn't move right away.

"Are you okay? Were you crying?" Giuseppe asked.

She headed straight for Giuseppe, who was closest, and hugged him around the waist. Giuseppe narrowed his eyes at Andreas with concern.

He mouthed the words "She's fine. Everything is okay now."

* * * *

Giuseppe cupped her cheeks, and she stepped back slightly, looking up into his eyes. Her gorgeous blue eyes sparkled with tears, her lips parted, and she stared up at him.

"I missed you," she said to him.

He squinted. She chuckled.

"Stupid?"

"Hell no. I missed you, too." Giuseppe pressed his lips to hers and kissed her tenderly. Giuseppe couldn't resist running his palm up under her shirt and against her back. The feel of some skimpy lace halter top had his curiosity on edge. She moaned into his mouth and pressed closer, and he slid his palm over her ass in the sexy pants she wore. She felt tight, hard, in shape, and her ass stuck out perfectly.

He pulled from her lips, and Dominick was there. He pressed his palm to her back. She looked up at him and smiled.

"Everything okay?" he asked.

She reached out and cupped his cheek. Giuseppe released her to his brother.

"It is now. It's perfect when I'm with the three of you. I'm sorry I didn't stay with you last night." She looked at Andreas. "Come here."

Now all three of them surrounded her close. She leaned back against Andreas, held Dominick's hand, and then took Giuseppe's hand and placed it against her chest. He could feel how full her breast was and how hard her heart pounded.

Tears filled her eyes. "I was scared last night, scared to feel what I was feeling, scared to let go and take what I wanted, what I knew was right and powerful, and I fought it. I couldn't sleep a wink last night. I tossed and turned and thought about Jimmy and about the three of you. This morning after class, I went to the cemetery in Brooklyn."

She looked at Andreas and smiled. "Andreas showed up as I expressed my fears, my desires, and the truth to Jimmy's grave. I needed to do it in order to let go, to move on, and to not feel guilty or like I was betraying him. I know you might not get it. I just had to do it. I don't want to fight what I feel for the three of you anymore. I know it's going to be crazy and dangerous, but I trust the three of you so much."

"You do?" Dominick asked, reached up, and cupped her cheek.

"So much," she whispered.

Dominick pressed closer and kissed her lips. Giuseppe winked at Andreas. When Dominick pulled from her mouth, he gave her a soft smile.

"We will give you whatever time you need, Giada. We won't rush you," Dominick told her.

She nibbled her bottom lip. "I'm not going to lie. I'm scared to make love again after all this time and with three large, dominant men like you. I want to be good for you. I want to please you and make the three of you so happy, but I'm not experienced or maybe what you're used to and can have whenever you want."

Giuseppe pressed a finger gently to her lips. "Sweetie, you're perfection. You're so damn special it's us who will worry about making you happy. Making you want to stay and be with us always."

Andreas clutched her shoulders, and she leaned back against him and looked from Giuseppe to Dominick.

"I'm ready. I want to be with the three of you."

Giuseppe's heart hammered inside of his chest when she stepped forward and began to undo the buttons on Giuseppe's shirt. As the material parted, she pressed her lips to his skin, and he closed his eyes and ran his hands up and down her arms, anticipating making love to her.

Giuseppe slid his hands down her arms to her hips and lifted her up and against him. She straddled his waist, and he tilted his head back at the same time she cupped his cheeks and pressed her lips to his.

She felt light, sexy, perfect in his arms as he carried her through the penthouse and toward the back bedroom.

* * * *

Giada was shaking, but she wouldn't let her fears, her inexperience stop her from giving herself to these men. So when

Giuseppe set her on her feet on the rug in front of the bed and stepped back to pull off his shirt the rest of the way, she spoke her mind.

"Oh God, you're beautiful," she whispered and couldn't help but reach out and caress his tanned skin. She felt her breathing grow rapid at the sight of all his muscles, the tanned skin, and how much taller, bigger he was in comparison to her. It was intimidating and arousing.

He gripped her hand and then brought it to his mouth. He kissed her fingers. "You're the beautiful one."

She glanced at Dominick, who pulled off his shirt and started to get undressed. Andreas reached for her top. She helped him take it off of her. She wanted to lick her lips at the sight of all their muscles, the hardness of their bodies that screamed masculinity, capability, and power.

Andreas slid his finger along the lace material of her halter bra. "Very sexy," Andreas whispered, stroking his thumb along her nipple while slipping his forefinger under the material of her bra and lifting it up and over her head.

She gasped at the contact to her sensitive flesh, at the feel of his thick thumb stroking her very sensitive nipple, and then him removing her top as if desperate to see her naked. She wanted to look good, sexy, desirable for them. They were so big, and she was petite. Would they really like that about her? Her mind kept battling between feeling good from their touches and wondering if she was good enough. She wanted to please them so badly she was shaking.

Her large breasts slipped from the material, and immediately Dominick cupped one and Giuseppe cupped the other one. Her lips parted from the feel of their big, warm hands cupping her like this and instantly. She watched in anticipation and awe as they lowered their mouths to her breasts and feasted on her.

"Oh my God. Oh," she moaned softly.

Her arms were still raised in the air by Andreas, and she locked gazes with him as she moaned.

"You're gorgeous." He slowly tossed her top to the side.

As she lowered her arms she held on to Dominick's and Giuseppe's heads and couldn't help but press them harder to her breasts, loving and needing more from them. She was entirely too turned on, and things were just getting started. Could she survive this? These sensations of arousal brought on triple time? Holy crap.

Andreas reached for her hips as he bent down to slide her bottoms down her legs. She'd stepped from the boots and her bottoms when she felt the finger tap at her belly ring while lips trailed from her breasts to her ribs on either side.

Three sets of hands smoothed over her skin there. Three extra-large men encased her, invaded her space and making her feel what claustrophobia had to feel like, but enjoyable instead of fearful.

"Goddamn, baby, you are hot," Dominick told her, lifted up, and pressed his mouth to hers.

She felt his palm slide along her hip to her ass and squeeze her. She moaned into his mouth and then tightened as she felt the lips press against her skin. She pulled from Dominick's lips to look down at Andreas. Wild, dominant Andreas.

She ran her fingers through his hair and pressed him closer to her. She gripped his hair with one hand as Dominick sucked on a sensitive chord on her neck. Behind her, Giuseppe kissed along her spine to her ass. It was all too much. Andreas sucked against her belly, making her giggle and then pull back and grip his cheeks. He looked up at her, and she smiled.

"Get ready, woman. You're going to be ours very soon."

He gripped her hips, lifted her, and lowered her to the bed. Andreas maneuvered between her legs, she slid her palms over Andreas's shoulders as he lowered over her, and he kissed her on the mouth. They explored one another with tongues, hands, and thrusts. When he released her lips to sit up, she reached for the buttons on his shirt, and when she spread the shirt wide, wanting, needing to feel his skin, she paused at what she saw.

Her heart hammered. Dominick and Giuseppe lay on either side of her and caressed her hair from her face as they kissed her shoulders and her arms.

"Andreas. Oh God." She smoothed her hands along the different scars. Some deep, some round, and others long like knife wounds. Tears escaped her eyes, and he gripped her cheeks and shook his head. She inhaled his cologne and his masculinity as well as the tension his cousins emitted at seeing Andreas's many scars. Her eyes widened. She blinked and thought about Jimmy, about how he hadn't survived being a soldier, and then about how Andreas had. She wondered what he had gone through and knew not to ask questions, to just love him and be thankful that he was alive and here with them today.

"Every night I hardly sleep thinking about all the shit I've done and survived. Wondered why the fuck I wasn't dead like so many of my friends, troops, family." He glanced at Dominick and Giuseppe and back at her. He looked at her body. "Now I know why. For you, baby. To protect you, to share you with Dominick and Giuseppe, and to love you."

She felt a tear escape from her eye, and she reached up and cupped his cheek. "I need you, Andreas. Now."

He lifted up, and she watched him undress the rest of the way while Dominick and Giuseppe explored her body. They slid their hands along her ankles then up her thighs to her pussy. They spread her wider, stroked thumbs and fingers along her clit. She gasped and tried to close her legs.

"No you don't. This sexy, curvy body is all ours to explore, to taste, and to possess." Dominick licked along her ribs to the tip of her breast and sucked the tiny bud into his mouth.

"Oh, Dominick." She moaned.

"From these cute, pink-painted toenails to this wet, bare pink pussy," Andreas said, lifting her foot and nipping her toes and ankle, calf, and thigh.

She giggled and tried pulling free, but then Giuseppe pressed a finger to her cunt, and she gasped. He pulled it back out, and she held his gaze. He licked his lips.

"You're already wet for us. I love it," he said to her.

Andreas continued sliding his hands from her ankles to her thighs, spreading her wider then teasing her cunt. He stroked her outer lips with his thumbs, and she stared at him, at his sexy, muscular body with all those dips and ridges, as well as his long, thick cock.

"She's so wet and tight. You're gripping my fingers, baby," Andreas said as he stroked her pussy.

"Let him in, Giada. Let go and give us complete control," Giuseppe said as he leaned up and kissed her mouth.

She immediately reached for him and ran her fingers through his hair as Andreas increased his finger thrusts. "Oh." She moaned again and felt her pussy cream.

"I need in. Now," Andreas said very firmly.

Giuseppe pulled back, and so did Dominick. Andreas reached for her hands and pressed them up above her head.

"Nice and easy, baby. You're on the pill still, right?" he asked.

"Yes." She knew they remembered because when they'd watched over her months ago they had had to pick up her prescriptions of birth control. She had been embarrassed, but part of her was happy they knew, especially now.

She held Andreas's gaze while he aligned his cock with her pussy. He kept his hands entwined with hers above her head. The tip of his thick cock pressed against her pussy. She shivered, felt anxious, nervous, excited, all rolled up in one.

"Nice and slow."

"I want you. I'm ready, Andreas. I am."

He gave a soft smirk and began to ease his cock into her cunt. He nudged and nudged. She held his gaze, felt the connection, the emotion as tears filled her eyes. She absorbed this moment, memorized the intense expressions of all three men, their muscular bodies, Andreas's tight abs, Giuseppe pinching her nipple, and Dominick stroking his cock and watching Andreas make love to her for the first time. It confirmed the fact that she would belong to all three men. That they would be one unit, one family, and she parted her lips and relaxed her muscles to let go and let him, them, in.

"Mine, forever." He pushed all the way into her. She gripped his hands and pushed upward as he pulled back again and then thrust all the way in. He began to stroke over and over again, and her pussy gushed cream, lubricating those strokes.

They exhaled.

"Oh God," she said.

"So fucking tight. Mercy, baby," he said through clenched teeth. He released her hands and slid his palms down her arms to her shoulders, gripping them and then using her shoulders as leverage to thrust in and out of her cunt.

"Andreas!" she cried out, unable to breathe when he stroked into her, his cock so thick and hard. She was panting and moaning, trying to take in the sight of him with all those muscles and how he towered over her. His hard, thick thighs had her legs spread as wide as they could go. He hammered into her cunt, and she felt that cramping sensation in her core and knew she was going to orgasm.

"Too tight. I needed you for too long, baby. I'm not going to last," he exclaimed.

She reached up and held onto his shoulders as he lowered and thrust faster, deeper into her. He was so big, so thick and hard, and then he sucked on her neck hard.

"Mine, now and forever," he said.

She came, aroused by his possessiveness and the dominant way he took her, claimed her body, and thrust into her so hard and deep.

"Yeah, Giada. Come all over my cock. Come for me. Fuck," he yelled out and came.

He crushed her as he hugged her tight and rolled to the side, sliding a hand over her ass and squeezing her. He kissed her cheeks, her chin, forehead, and her lips.

"Never ever like this, woman. Know that. Never like this," he said to her and continued to kiss her.

When he finally released her to pull back, he winked at Dominick, who was behind her. She looked over her shoulder just as Dominick cupped her breast and pulled her to him. He kissed her lips. Andreas released her to him, and then she rolled on top of Dominick to kiss him and explore his skin.

She kissed his lips, his neck, and his shoulder while he explored her ass with his hands. When she felt the second set of fingers slide over her ass and up the crack, she tightened, turned, and saw Giuseppe. He was stroking his cock. Dominick tapped her jaw, and she looked back down at him.

"This first time is going to be quick, love. Watching this ass, thinking about your sexy dancing, watching you submit to Andreas and let him love you have me about to shoot my load. Take me inside of you, Giada. Make me yours," Dominick said to her.

She lifted and aligned her pussy with his cock. She held his gaze and slid her palms up his muscular, tanned chest to his shoulders while sinking onto his cock. He gripped her wrists. His hips were wide, thick, and she felt feminine and small in comparison. Yet she wasn't scared they could hurt her. Their sizes turned her on. She missed being with a man and feeling protected. Being with these three men had her coming like a faucet. She looked at Dominick's large hands, absorbed how they felt encasing her small wrists. She couldn't help but take in everything about each of these men. It had seemed like it had been forever since she'd felt a man's intimate touch or the way it felt to be held, controlled, and made love to. Her eyes welled up with tears.

"No. No, no, no, lover. No ghosts, no past, just the present and future with us," Dominick said to her as if reading her mind.

She smiled, leaned down, kissed his lips, and took pleasure in tasting them, teasing him as she slowly moved up and down on his shaft. He gripped her hips and thrust upward, indicating that she was going too slow and he needed more. It gave her confidence that she had what it took to make this man—these men—wild with desire for her body. She gripped his shoulders, and then he ran his large hands up and down her arms. His eyes swept over her breasts, and it was as if he'd touched them. They reacted, and she began to ride his cock. He gripped her hips.

"So feminine and petite. You need protection, love. You need looking after."

She must have been going too slow because suddenly he was staring at her, his eyes narrowed as though he was thinking about something, and then he rolled her onto her back and began to stroke into her cunt fast and deep with his large hands gripping her hips tightly.

She could hardly catch her breath. "Dominick. Oh God, Dominick!"

"Mine. No other men ever. No one fucks this body, touches this body but us. Understand me? No one," he exclaimed loudly.

"Yes, Dominick. Only you, Andreas, and Giuseppe. Only the three of you ever," she told him, and she felt her body erupt. "Oh." She moaned.

He stroked into her harder, faster, pressing her arms above her head, and she locked onto his eyes. The veins protruded from his temples. His teeth were clenched, and his nostrils flared.

"Ours. Finally, all ours," he exclaimed. "Giada!" he yelled out, and then he thrust and stroked into her so hard and fast, as though he were trying to mark her and claim her as his woman, that she came again as she hugged him tight.

* * * *

Giuseppe pulled Giada into his arms and kissed her tenderly. "Are you okay? Not too sore?"

She stroked his cheeks and smiled. "Take me, Giuseppe. Make love to me next and make me your woman." She kissed his lips.

He kissed her back, and they explored their bodies with hands and mouths. His large, firm hand caressed her ass and squeezed it tight. His other hand smoothed up her back, gripped her hair, and tightened his hold as he plunged his tongue into her mouth in exploration and possession. She moaned and rocked her hips, more than ready to make love to Giuseppe next.

He pulled from her lips and sucked on her neck and then her breasts, pulling, tugging on her oversensitive nipple. She gripped his shoulders. "Make me yours, Giuseppe. Please, I need you." She begged for him to make love to her.

"You're already mine." He winked, then lifted, gripped her hips, and turned her onto her belly.

She gasped, and he slapped his hands together.

"Goddamn, I knew you had a fabulous ass, baby. I'm going to do a little exploring because, later today, the three of us are going to take you together." He massaged her ass with both hands and then up her back to her shoulders.

"Oh God, Giuseppe. I don't know if I'm ready." She moaned.

Smack.

"Ouch," she exclaimed.

Then he stroked a finger into her cunt and found her wet. "Oh yeah, you'll be ready. One spank and you're coming."

He gripped her hips, pulled her to the edge of the bed, and leaned over her back. He sucked on her skin by her neck while he caressed her. He kissed and licked her skin as he used his hands to massage her muscles. He spread her arms above her head so she was flat to the mattress as he eased down, taking his time to explore every inch of her. A lick to her shoulder and nip to her ribs, she giggled and moved her hips. He gave her ass a light tap, and it somehow turned her on further. She moaned and exhaled, feeling her body begin to relax, and then his tongue licked along the crack of her ass then lower.

"Giuseppe." She moaned.

When he chuckled, his warm breath collided with her puckered hole. "Mine," he said to her.

She exhaled and relaxed her muscles.

* * * *

Giuseppe continued exploring her to absorb how it felt to finally possess Giada Slane, the one woman who'd turned their world upside down.

"You feel incredible in my arms, underneath me in bed where you belong," he said, sliding his hands along her hips bones to her ass cheeks, spreading them, and massaging them before he lowered and then nipped her skin. She eased her ass back against him. She as so small and sexy that he could encase her whole body and cover her almost entirely. That made him feel possessive and very, very protective.

He lifted her hips. "On all fours. Just like this."

She gripped the comforter, and he spread her thighs. He stood at the edge of the bed just looking at her body and ran his palms up her thighs to her back. He glanced at Dominick and Andreas. Their facial expressions were filled with lust and a seriousness he felt, as well.

This wasn't just sex. This was more—way more. He felt it everywhere and in places he didn't want to admit could be penetrated. This sexy, petite woman was a weapon of mass destruction against them, and that made him nervous and have a need to dominate and control.

He was breathing through his nostrils as he eased a palm under her belly and straight to her breast. He cupped it, using his thumb to stroke her nipple.

"Oh, Giuseppe."

Then he eased back, looking at her perfect, flawless skin, and slid a finger along her spine, down her ass, over the crack, and into her cunt.

"Oh yeah. Wet, tight, ready for me, aren't you, love?" he asked and stroked a little faster. He was trying to go slow, but really he wanted to go fast, to fuck her so hard, so deeply that she would never be the same woman again and always know she belonged to him, to Dominick and Andreas. It was barbaric, but it was how he felt.

She started to rock her hips.

"Nice, Giada," Andreas chimed in, lying on the side of the bed and stroking her cheek. She parted her lips, and Andreas pressed his finger to her mouth. She sucked it in.

"Oh, I think our woman is really going to enjoy pleasing us and taking all our cocks into her body at once," Dominick now added, joining them on the bed, stroking her hair and moving her head back and forth as though she was sucking Andreas's cock, not his finger.

"So hot," Giuseppe whispered and stroked the finger from her cunt to her ass, applying just a little pressure to her puckered hole with his thick thumb. Back and forth he spread her cream, and she moaned and moved a little faster. When he slid his finger into her ass, she let go of Andreas's finger.

"Oh God. Oh, Giuseppe."

"That's it, baby," Giuseppe said and then inched his cock closer to her cunt and slid into her pussy from behind.

"Oh."

They both moaned. He pulled his finger from her ass and gripped her hips. "She is more than ready." He stroked into her pussy from behind in rapid thrusts. He leaned over her and gripped her hair, his thighs slapping against her ass and thighs.

"Who do you belong to, Giada? Who?"

"You. Oh!"

Her head tilted back, her breasts pushed forward, and Giuseppe's cock, all the way in her cunt, filled her. He thrust again and again, rocked his hips, and felt her tighten and then scream out as she came. Giuseppe sucked on her neck.

"Oh God, I can't. Oh, too much. Too much," she exclaimed.

"Never too much. You have three lovers now, woman. You need training," Andreas added, then slid under her, and began to feast on her other breast.

She cried out and shook as she came, sending Giuseppe over the edge. He thrust a few more times and then followed, unable to hold off, the sensations overwhelming.

He pulled out of her and lifted her into his arms. She clung to him and kissed him everywhere her lips could reach. His cheeks, his lips, and then his neck. He lowered her and rose above her so he couldn't crush Giada with his weight. He held her face between his hands and stared down into her gorgeous blue eyes.

"Only the beginning, baby. By the time we get through with you, you'll never want to be away from us—not ever." He pressed his lips to hers, and she hugged him tight.

Chapter 8

Giada awoke to the feel of warm lips kissing along her shoulder and back. Her face was wedged up against Giuseppe's chest, her arm over his waist, her breast against his skin. The lips continued trailing along her spine then to her ass. She moaned softly.

"She's awake. We didn't kill her," Andreas teased as he continued exploring her.

Giuseppe chuckled. "No way. Not our woman. She was made for us." Giuseppe stroked her arm that lay over his waist. She opened her eyes to look up at him.

"So it wasn't a dream?" she asked.

"Hell no, honey."

He winked, and she gasped as Andreas's tongue licked along the crack of her ass as he spread her thighs, lifting it up over Giuseppe's thigh. Giuseppe grabbed onto it and held her under her knee. She moaned again as Andreas sucked on her cunt and then licked back and forth over her anus. She was curious about them taking her there. Was it too soon? Was it automatically expected with three lovers? Oh God, the idea aroused her but scared her. Once they took her there, it somehow would make this more real, more intimate, and a sign of possession for them. She realized she wanted them to. She wanted to be claimed in every way, and then she lifted and realized that Dominick wasn't there.

"He'll be back soon. Had to take care of business." Giuseppe said.

Andreas stroked fingers into her cunt. She nodded and noticed Giuseppe's cock lift, all hard and aroused. She slid to the left. He thought she was going to resist Andreas's ministrations, and he gripped her knee, only for her to lower and hold his gaze.

"I want to taste you, Giuseppe."

His eyes darkened, his hold loosened, and she slid between his legs, cupped his balls, and licked his cock while she spread her legs wider and lifted, giving Andreas fuller access to her body.

Andreas jumped up from the bed. "You are such a sight, woman. Your hair is so long and beautiful." Andreas gripped her hair, pulling it to one side and over her shoulder.

Giuseppe held on to it, spread his thighs, and tilted his hips upward, thrusting into her mouth.

Andreas leaned over her. "You trust us? You belong to us now, in every way." He slid a wet digit along her anus and pushed in.

She tightened up and moaned but continued to suck on Giuseppe's cock. Giuseppe stroked her hair and gripped it.

"You've got an incredible mouth, Giada. Fucking incredible, woman." He thrust upward.

She was pleasing them, making them happy, and that was what she wanted. She heard the door open.

"What do we have here?" Dominick asked.

She couldn't look to where he was, not with Giuseppe thrusting his cock into her mouth.

"I think our woman is ready for the three of us to take her together. We need to make this official, Dominick. Grab the lube," Andreas said.

Dominick slid his hand along her back. She moaned. "Such a seductress. Holy fuck do I love watching you suck Giuseppe's cock." Dominick stroked her hair and then her back and her ass.

"She has my dick super hard, man. I want into this ass, and now," Andreas stated.

Dominick snickered. "Don't we all, man. I'll grab the lube. Get her into position," Dominick ordered.

It all aroused her so much that when Andreas pulled his fingers from her ass and Giuseppe gripped her hair and asked her to release his cock, she felt disappointed but also curious as to what they were up to.

"We're taking you together. This makes it official, honey. Tell me, have you ever had a cock in your ass?" Giuseppe asked.

"No. Never."

"Okay then. Nice and slow."

He pulled her down to kiss him. Behind her, she could hear drawers opening, and then Giuseppe released her lips.

"Slide on down to the edge of the bed," Giuseppe told her.

"Wait. I need something from her first," Dominick said, now naked and standing by the edge of the bed.

He reached for her, lifted her into his arms, and kissed her. She ran her fingers through his hair and over the muscles on his chest as he ran his hands along her body possessively. When he finally got his fill, he held her gaze.

"Don't resist. Just relax all these muscles and let us in. We'll go slow." He looked at her breasts, cupped one, and thumbed the nipple. "Well, as slow as we can. Your body drives us insane, woman. Insane." He tugged on her nipple, making her gasp.

* * * *

Giuseppe lay on the edge of the bed, legs wide and stroking his cock, Andreas grabbed the lube, and Dominick placed Giada over Giuseppe, who took her into his arms and kissed her. She lifted, aligned her pussy with his cock, and slid right onto his shaft.

Andreas watched, stared at her body and ran his hands along her skin from shoulders to hips. She was feminine, soft, delicate, and he didn't want to hurt her. Dominick gave him a tap.

"She'll be okay. Nice and slow," he said to him.

Andreas licked his lips.

Dominick moved onto the bed. "You are gorgeous and all ours." Dominick stroked her hair and then kissed her.

Giuseppe cupped her breasts and rocked his hips. "So fucking wet, too. I think our woman wants the three of us."

"Do you, baby?" Dominick asked, cupping her cheeks.

"Yes. I want to try. Will it hurt?"

"Maybe a little at first, but we'll get you ready. Andreas knows what to do. You come first, always, love. Always," Dominick said and pressed his lips to hers.

As they kissed, Andreas slid a lubed finger against her ass, and she tightened, but then Giuseppe slowed his thrusts, allowing her body to get used to double penetration.

In and out he thrust his lubed finger into her ass in time with Giuseppe's strokes. Dominick brought her lower to suck his cock, and the moment he heard Dominick exhale, he knew she was sucking him down. It aroused Andreas, made him feel possessive and protective of their woman. That thought that she was truly theirs to love, to cherish, and protect tugged at his core and his soul.

"I need in, baby. Show me you're ready for me, too."

She pushed her ass back against his fingers and rocked her hips over Giuseppe's cock.

"She is more than ready. I'm almost there. This mouth is so sensual. Fuck," Dominick said.

Andreas was shaking. He'd never felt like this before, so worried about hurting a woman, taking her so intimately with his cousins like this. It was different and powerful. When he eased fingers out of her ass and replaced them with the tip of his cock, he absorbed the moment—the sight of her naked body, Dominick gripping her hair and thrusting his cock into her mouth, Giuseppe lifting his hips upward, and her ass rocking back and forth. Her anus tapped against his cock, and he couldn't wait. He needed, wanted, to claim her like this.

As he eased into her ass, sliding through the tight rings, nudging and nudging until he slipped all the way in, he exhaled. "Holy fuck," he exclaimed. He gripped her hips, and they all moaned.

"Slow down, Giada, or I'll come. My brother needs to move," Dominick complained, and Giuseppe grunted.

"Move, Andreas, fucking move. She's too tight. My cock is going to explode," Giuseppe complained.

Andreas pulled out and slammed back into her ass. The sensations were overwhelming, and he gave in to the need, the desires of all of them. In and out he thrust into her ass.

Dominick yelled out. "Swallow me, Giada," he demanded through clenched teeth as he came. When he released his seed, Dominick pulled from her mouth and slid from the bed.

Giada cried out, "Oh God. Oh my God." She came hard, shaking, gasping for breath.

"Fuck yeah. Never like this. Fuck." Giuseppe grunted and thrust superfast up and down as she fell against Giuseppe's chest. Andreas kept up, stroking into her ass over and over again, and then he and Giuseppe came. He fell over them but used his arms to hold himself somewhat up above them. Giada was breathing heavily, and so was Giuseppe. He was kissing her cheeks and her face and holding her against his chest. Andreas slowly pulled out of her ass and kissed along her spine and then rubbed her thighs.

Dominick returned with a washcloth and towel and began to wash her as Giuseppe rolled her to her side. They cleaned her up, and Andreas slid between her legs, cupped her cheek, and stared at her flushed skin and her naked body, feminine and gorgeous.

"Did we hurt you?" he asked.

She shook her head. "I think I blacked out."

Giuseppe chuckled and cupped her breast. "Damn you know how to inflate a man's ego."

Andreas smiled down at her. "I don't think we'll ever let you out of this bed."

She blushed. "Maybe it's me who won't let the three of you out of this bed."

"Oh really?" Dominick stated with his hands on his hips.

"I don't think so. You need to learn who is in charge," Giuseppe said and started tickling her. She laughed and rolled into Giuseppe, and Andreas got up and gave her ass a smack.

"Andreas," she scolded.

He raised one eyebrow up at her and pointed. "I own this ass now. Remember that. And my brothers are next."

* * * *

Andreas walked down the hall as the others showered and got ready for some dinner. His cell phone buzzed, and Train apologized for disturbing them but mentioned someone going to Giada's apartment looking for her.

He walked out of the penthouse and to the guards' quarters. "What's going on?" he asked, his hair still wet from his shower.

"We took care of it," Royce said to him.

"Who went to her apartment?" he asked, snapping at them. He didn't mean to, but he felt even more possessive of her now that they'd made love and taken her together. He crossed his arms in front of his chest, and Train cleared his throat.

"It was her Uncle Les," Train told him.

Andreas uncrossed his arms and narrowed his eyes. "What?"

"Yeah, he showed up, and Toby told him she wasn't home. He demanded to know who he was, and he told him he worked for you and your cousins. Toby told him to go home and that she was safe and with you guys."

"Good.'

"Not really, Andreas. He showed up here an hour ago," Logic said and smirked.

"Are you kidding me? To do what? Make her leave us and rant about his bullshit?" Andreas asked.

"Pretty much, but he was a little drunk. I smelled the alcohol, and I had one of the guys drop him off at home."

Andreas exhaled.

"This guy going to be a problem between you guys and your woman?" Royce asked him.

"I won't let it be. I'll have to talk to her, though, and let Giada know."

"If he comes back?" Train asked.

"Let me know. Any other updates on the deliveries Sunny and the guys did?" he asked Royce.

"All went smoothly, and Vinny took care of sending that message to Calvarro," Royce added.

"Good. Now we wait and see. I suppose if anyone is going to get any shit from that it will be the Fiorres and Costanzas since Sunny and Major did the job themselves."

"Not necessarily," Royce told him.

"What do you mean?"

"Those men, Calvarro, Alajandro, and Toro, had their eyes on Giada. Still do." He squinted at Royce, and Royce nodded to Logic, who passed over Giada's purse.

"She left this in the SUV. We brought it up earlier. The thing's been going off a lot," Logic told him.

He looked inside of her black purse and took out her cell phone. He saw the list of text messages. He couldn't read whole texts but got the gist of it. All from Toro, Alajandro, Calvarro, and Uncle Les.

"What the fuck?" he asked.

"Hey, I mean no disrespect, boss, but do you think maybe Giada fooled around with them or something to make those men pursue her? I mean obviously she didn't sleep with them. We know why she waited to accept you guys," Royce said. He was a loyal man and friend. They all were.

"As much as it pisses me off to think about that, we all could tell they were making moves. None of it matters now. Giada is our woman. We'll do what we need to protect her. I'll make certain there's nothing else for us to know." Andreas was angry and jealous. He was going to confront her about this as soon as he headed back into the penthouse.

"We ordered food. It will be here shortly," Brew said.

"Thanks." He headed back to the penthouse with her bag and cell phone.

* * * *

Giada put on one of the guys' dress shirts. She rolled up the sleeves and was going to put on her pants when Andreas entered the bedroom. He looked pissed off as he tossed her purse onto the bed and held her phone.

"How intimate did you get with Toro and Alajandro?" he questioned her, shocking her.

He was angry, and with one look at her phone, she realized that something had set him off. "What do you mean?"

"Goddamn it, Giada. It's a simple fucking question. I realize you didn't fuck them, but how much did you fool around with them? Did you let them kiss you? Touch you? Pleasure you?" he demanded.

Then Dominick and Giuseppe came out wearing pants and dress shirts.

"What's going on?" Dominick asked.

She felt the tears hit her eyes.

"Read these fucking texts, ones from Toro and Alajandro wanting to see her again, kiss her, spend time with her."

Dominick took the phone.

"I didn't let them touch me or pleasure me," she said to him.

"They kissed you? Felt you up?" he demanded, stepping closer.

She didn't move, couldn't move. "I was unaware of who they were then. I was trying to—"

"Push us away and deny your feelings so you allowed them to touch you and kiss you?" Giuseppe demanded to know now, too.

She couldn't lie to them. Plus, it had been before them, before she knew who Toro and Alajandro were. "We kissed, it got a little heavy, and I stopped them from coming into my apartment. Nothing else happened."

Andreas growled and clenched his fists by his side. She went to move toward him, and Giuseppe stopped her and shook his head.

She was scared. In that moment, she realized that Andreas had a side to him that she didn't want to know about. She also wasn't about to be controlled or accused of doing something she didn't do. They hadn't been together then. What about women they had been with and screwed? Was she supposed to bring them up now and be angry about them?

She slid Dominick's hand away and raised her voice to Andreas. "What about you? The three of you? And all the women you've fooled around with, kissed, seduced into bed, and fucked? Am I supposed to bring them up now and question you about them? Be jealous of those who were before me and what we shared today?"

Andreas was in a dead stare with her. Dominick placed his hands on his hips.

"We didn't seduce you and just fuck you." Dominick was now pissed off.

"Hmm." She went to walk away, but Andreas grabbed her wrist and pulled her into his arms. He lifted her and then lowered her onto the bed. He stared into her eyes, and she gulped.

"I know they want you. I care about you so much, need you so much that I feel possessive and protective of you. So when I see text messages from men who want to fuck my woman, I see red, Giada, fucking red," he said through clenched teeth.

She stared into his dark eyes, and she nodded her head. "I understand. That's something you'll need to work on so we don't fight for no reason."

He narrowed his eyes at her. "What?"

She had only gotten to button two buttons on the dress shirt when Andreas came storming into the room. She undid the buttons while holding his gaze. She pushed the material apart. "I belong to you, Giuseppe, and Dominick. No one else. This body is yours, Andreas. Now kiss me because, for some crazy reason, your barbaric, controlling temper is turning me on, and I need you."

"Jesus," Giuseppe exclaimed.

"Fucking insane," Dominick said as Andreas loomed over her, used one hand to cup her breast, and eased his hand up her neck and under her hair while he lowered down and kissed her. In a flash that kiss grew wild, and seconds later, after some maneuvering and moaning, his pants were down and off of him, his cock was fisted in his hand, and he held her gaze.

"Damn straight this body is ours. No other men ever again, or I'll kill them."

Andreas thrust into her pussy, making her moan aloud and grip onto his shoulders. He wrapped her up, pulled her to the edge of the bed, and thrust into her fast and repeatedly while his cousins left the room, giving them the time they needed to resolve this issue.

She ran her fingers through his hair as he nipped her neck and sucked hard on her collarbone. "I love you, Andreas. I don't know if you realize that if you heard me earlier today."

He stroked faster. He kissed her lips, her cheek, and her neck. His mouth was next to her ear. "I heard everything, Giada, everything. I love you, too, and I promise this won't be the last time I get jealous or need to make love to you and ensure this is real and you are mine."

"I'm sure it won't be, but remember, Andreas, you belong to only me, too. You won't want to see a jealous side of me, not ever."

He chuckled. She felt his cock harden.

"You just threaten a made man, a soldier?"

"Not a threat, lover, a promise. Now make me come, Andreas. Make me beg for mercy."

"Holy fuck." He lifted and pulled her lower so her ass was off the edge of the bed and her shoulders were the only part of her on the mattress. He pounded into her, watching her breasts bounce, and she watched his eyes close as she shook and came and he followed.

"Mine always, Giada. Always."

She smiled as he lowered and hugged her tight, and they remained that way until her belly rumbled and he laughed against her chest.

"Let's eat then head back to bed for the night. I think it's going to take several times making love to you to stop the jealous thoughts running through my head," he said, stroking the hair from her cheek and staring down into her eyes.

"Okay, Andreas. Perhaps if all three of you take me together it may help." She winked.

He snickered. "Oh really? Someone likes a cock in every hole, does she?" he teased and tickled her as he rose.

"I like all three of my men inside of me, making love to me. It was amazing, Andreas. I can't believe I let you do that."

He stroked her jaw. "Believe it. We're one now. We will protect you and teach you what it's going to be like to be the woman of made men. Something tells me you'll be just fine."

He lifted and offered her his hand. She got up and ran her fingers through her damp tendrils. "I need to wash up."

"Okay. I'll wait with Giuseppe and Dominick. You may want to get dressed in case the others join us. I don't want them seeing my woman's body."

She nodded. "Glad you told me. I was thinking of coming out naked," she teased.

"Sure you were. You talk a big talk, but we know how shy and reserved you are. It's part of your appeal. Sweet, feminine, and precious." He gave her ass a tap. "Go wash up."

She smiled and headed into the bathroom, her heart full of love and happiness as she freshened up.

This could really work.

Chapter 9

Sunny looked at Roman, one of Fedarro's guards.

"I don't know why, but that seemed too easy," Sunny said to him as they drove through the dark streets after hitting one of Calvarro's warehouses. There had been only three guards on duty. It was a small place, but it did hold a good amount of merchandise belonging to Calvarro. It was now up in flames. See how he liked losing a hundred grand in merchandise.

"I know. I get that same feeling, and I don't like it," Roman said.

"Everyone got out, though. All our guys, and we cleared them all," Sunny said.

"What the hell is that?" Roman asked as they headed along the street when they both noticed something in the middle of the road. He slowed down.

"Be careful. It might be a trap or some shit," Sunny said.

As Roman got closer, he saw it was a body. Then it moved. "Shit, that's Felix. He's one of our informants who helped with this operation tonight." Roman stopped the SUV. He got out, gun drawn, and looked around them.

Sunny did the same thing. "Is he alive?"

"He's been shot. It looks bad."

"Let's get him into the back and get him help," Sunny said, and they quickly loaded him into the back of the SUV. "Who did this to you?" Sunny asked him.

"I didn't see his face." He moaned, and Sunny looked at Roman.

"Was it one of Calvarro's guys?" Roman asked.

"I don't think so." He moaned again.

"Okay, just relax, Felix. We're going to get you help," Roman said, and then, as they got him comfortable in the back of the SUV, shots were fired at them.

"What the fuck?"

"Get in," Roman yelled at Sunny, who jumped into the back with Felix as Roman ran around the other side, got in on the passenger side, slid over the seat, and took off driving.

Bullets hit the windows, breaking the glass, and tires squealed as they got the hell out of there.

"What the fuck? They tried to kill us," Roman yelled out.

"They let us escape," Sunny said, pulled out his cell phone, and called Fedarro. He wasn't sure who'd come after them, but he would find out, and when he did, they were dead.

* * * *

After they ate dinner along with their men, Giada walked over and looked at her cell phone.

"What did they say in the texts?" Giuseppe asked.

Dominick was concerned and jealous, too. She was their woman.

"Well, they want to schedule another meeting. Dinner or lunch at Rinaldi's."

"Dicks," Royce said, and she looked at him.

"What?"

"Rinaldi's is where men take a woman on a date to impress her and then expect her to put out," he said to her.

"We went there for a business meeting," she said to him.

He raised his hands up as if saying that didn't matter.

"Well, they didn't succeed in landing her. What else does it say?" Giuseppe asked.

She swallowed hard. "Just small talk." She lowered the phone.

"I'll have to figure out a way to make the meeting take place at the office so it's more official," she said.

Giuseppe took her hand and the phone. "Small talk? Just read it, or I will. Remember we gave you the opportunity to look at the texts and read them to us. We didn't have to," he scolded.

She looked intimidated. She worried her bottom lip. "They probably said these things thinking you were going to see them."

"Read them," Andreas ordered.

She looked at the cell phone. "'Maybe we can go dancing again. I dream about the feel of your hips under my hands...' I don't need to read this."

"Give me that." Giuseppe pulled the phone from her hand and stood up. "Fucking scumbag." He scrolled down. "No private meetings. We'll make the call and let them know they see her for business with one of us present or not at all," Giuseppe said firmly.

"That bad?" Brew asked.

He handed him her cell phone.

"Why does it matter what they say? They know I'm with the three of you. What am I going to do about work? I can't back out or try to tell my boss that I can't fulfill a contract because my boyfriends are jealous."

"It's not just being jealous. It's knowing that they want you. They want to play fucking games with us," Giuseppe stated.

Dominick's cell phone rang, and so did Royce's. They both walked to the side. Dominick answered. It was Fedarro.

"We got a problem, and another possible person pissed with our new business venture."

"What do you mean?"

"Someone tried to kill Sunny, Roman, and Felix."

"What?" He raised his voice, and all commotion over the texts stopped, and he looked at Royce.

"I'm on with Roman." Royce walked from the room.

"What's going on?" Andreas asked.

Dominick held up his hand as Fedarro explained. "No idea who then?"

"None, Dominick," Fedarro stated.

"What do you think you want to do?"

"Contact Calvarro and set up that meeting. He needs to know where we stand and what his choices are—realistically."

"Understood. Want me to make the call?"

"No. Considering that you're with Giada right now and have been all day, I think it wiser that I make the arrangements."

"Okay. Keep us posted. Will Felix be okay?"

"Yes."

"And Sunny?"

"Fine, just pissed off like Roman is. I know Roman is speaking with Royce. They'll get organized and have you covered as necessary."

"Thanks. We'll take the necessary precautions. Let me know what else you need. We have to identify the ones responsible before we threaten to take them out."

"That is what we need to work on. I'll be in touch," Fedarro said, and Dominick disconnected the call.

Everyone was quiet, and Dominick looked at Brew.

"Brew, stay here with Giada while we take care of something down the hall." Brew nodded.

"What's going on?" Giada asked.

Giuseppe stood up. "No questions," he said firmly.

She pulled her bottom lip between her teeth. They all left the kitchen and penthouse.

Dominick started to explain the situation to Andreas and Giuseppe.

"They're okay, though?" Giuseppe asked.

"Yes."

"No leads. Do they think it was Calvarro?" Andreas asked.

"No leads, and they don't think it was him, but someone Calvarro knows because they knew Sunny and Roman and the crew were at the warehouse," Dominick stated.

"An inside job? Fuck, I don't like that," Andreas stated.

"Let's not jump to conclusions," Dominick said, and they gathered in the small meeting room. "Let's get organized and keep in contact with Fedarro and Sunny. When they confirm a meeting place, time and location, we have to plan to be on alert and ready for anything—anything."

They all agreed. He thought not only about Giada and how he was going to keep her safe but also about how to make her understand that their business was none of her business. The sooner she learned the rules, the better off she would be.

* * * *

Giada was sitting in the living room with Brew. The men hadn't come back in yet. She felt funny, sort of out of place. She looked at her cell phone and at her e-mail account. She exhaled.

"Problem?" he asked.

"I should know better than to open up my e-mail on the weekend. Looks like I'll be swamped at work this week." She scrolled through the e-mail from her boss about the meeting with another new potential client. She supposed it was probably good to not see an e-mail or a get a phone call that she was fired or in danger of losing the new position because of Alajandro and Toro. Perhaps there was a way to salvage this situation, and maybe when she did speak with them, she would explain that things had happened and she didn't have feelings for them. She thought about the night both men had kissed her and about how she'd panicked.

Then she thought about Andreas's jealousy and about how angry he was. It made her think about their reaction to the phone call from Fedarro and whatever business they were conducting, business she couldn't know about, yet they planned to know everything about her business. Was this a potentially disastrous situation? Would she have to quit her job? She'd worked so hard for it. She worried her bottom lip when her cell phone rang. She gasped, and Brew narrowed his eyes. "Who is it?"

"Uncle Les."

"Don't answer it," he told her and sat forward.

She squinted at him. "Why?"

"Just don't."

"He could need me. He was in some sort of trouble a couple of weeks ago." She answered the call anyway, ignoring Brew's request, and he didn't look happy. Was she supposed to obey their guards' orders, too? "Hello?"

"Where are you? Tell me you aren't with the Coglonie men."

"Uncle Les, what do you want?"

"You need to get away from them. They're trouble, and they mean you harm."

She swallowed hard and held her fingers against the bridge of her nose, feeling a headache begin. "They aren't going to hurt me."

"Please, Giada, listen to me. You need to get away from them. Go back to your apartment."

"No. I'm with them now. I'm not going to argue about this. It isn't any of your business."

"It is my business. They'll use you. Put you in danger. Make you quit your job and control your life. Is that what you want?"

Tears stung her eyes. She looked at Brew.

"Hang up on him," he said.

"Who said that? One of them? See what I mean. Don't listen to their lies. They're bad men. They were involved in something tonight. I heard that people were killed in a fire they set and others shot."

Her eyes widened.

"Hang up on him now."

"I don't believe you." She felt the tears hit her eyes, and Brew got up off the couch. "I need to go." She ended the call, covered her mouth with her hand, and wondered what the hell she was going to do about Uncle Les. Was he drunk, in trouble, or just looking to start an argument with her over the Coglonie men? What?

"Giada?"

She shook her head. "I'm fine." She tried not to talk. She was emotional. She wanted to be happy right now, overjoyed to be with her three men, and instead, they were out of the room conducting business she wasn't allowed to know anything about, and she had to sit here and be obedient. Her uncle had called to warn her away from three men she loved already, and now the evening was ruined. Her mind began to process the effects that this type of relationship would bring her—isolation from others, eventually losing her job because, how could she do her job if her men, their guards, would need to be present? Her clients would be alarmed and uncomfortable. Her men wouldn't allow her to wine and dine potential clients, especially men. Her life would change. She would need to readjust, but they would go on their way. She stood up and paced the room.

"You're freaking out," Brew said to her.

She looked at him. "I'm processing things." She gulped and wiped her eyes. Was she the right woman for them? For this type of life? Would she have to quit her job? She loved her job. She loved finance and banking. How could it work if they would keep her on a short chain? No, leash. It would be a leash. Her uncle had warned her of the relationship with made men. She would become a prisoner, their slave, their woman to control and…the tears fell.

"Giada?"

Giuseppe entered the room, squinting. Brew stood up. "Her uncle Les called her. He's displeased she is here." Brew stepped aside.

Giuseppe looked at her. "He doesn't matter. You don't really even have a relationship with him, do you?"

"He knows I would help him, Giuseppe."

"I thought you weren't talking to him once we were providing security for you when Rayanna was missing. He stayed away."

"You threatened him," she said.

"Warned him that we could protect you better than he could," Giuseppe countered.

"He doesn't mean any harm."

Brew raised his eyebrows at her, and she lowered her eyes. Giuseppe walked closer.

"He's trouble. He can't just show up at your apartment and demand to see you like he did earlier. If he comes here and makes a scene, my guards will remove him."

"He isn't trouble. He's had it rough."

"And you're always there to bail him out. When was the last time you even saw him?" Giuseppe asked her.

She hesitated to answer.

"Giada, the truth, nothing less, remember?" Giuseppe ordered with his hands on his hips. He was in a mood. Whatever had taken place had angered him.

"He got into some sort of fight. I had to go pick him up because he was in bad shape."

"When was this?" Brew asked.

"Two weeks ago. It was late when I got the call from the bartender at Govan's."

"Govan's? That's a fucking dive and in a bad neighborhood. What fucking night and time was it?" Brew asked, seeming just as angry at her as Giuseppe was.

"I don't remember, but it was fine. I got there, and we took a cab to Queens, and then I headed home. He's the only family I have, Giuseppe, so I try." She saw the way Brew looked at Giuseppe.

Giuseppe exhaled. "That is never going to happen again. He calls you, needs to talk or meet or is in trouble, then you tell one of us, Brew, or the others. Whoever is with you."

"About that. How are we going to work this out?"

"Work what out?"

"Security. I need privacy with my clients and working. I can't have someone with me all the time. I'll get fired."

Giuseppe looked at Brew, and Brew nodded and walked toward the door to the penthouse. Giuseppe eyed her over. "We need to figure it out."

"I'm concerned. I won't be ordered around or treated like I'm below all of you and have no rights or no say in anything. I won't. I've worked too hard to get my position, and now there's this new liaison position, and I'll have to meet with potential clients. I can't do that with a bunch of oversized, gun-carrying bouncers around me."

"Slow down." He pulled her into his arms. She stared up at him, and he smiled softly. "We'll work it out, and for the record, if you want the guys to like you, I wouldn't ever refer to them as oversized, gun-carrying bouncers to their faces."

She gave his arm a slap. "I like them, and I wouldn't. I'm just frazzled from Uncle Les's call. The things he said just bothered me."

"What did he say?" he asked and took her over to the couch. He pulled her onto his lap so she had to straddle his hips.

He started caressing up her sweater and along her ribs, making her lose focus. "He just warned me to stay clear of you guys, said I was making a mistake," she whispered.

His eyes narrowed. "He's wrong, and he's too late." Giuseppe cupped her breast with one hand, eased his other toward her back and neck, and pulled her closer.

"Who do you belong to, baby?" he asked, staring at her lips.

Her belly fluttered, and her heart raced. "You."

He pressed his lips to hers and plunged his tongue into her mouth. He lowered her to the side of the couch, pushed up her top, slid her lace bra over, and captured her breast with his mouth. He tugged and sucked hard. She moaned and stared at his mouth then his eyes as they locked onto hers. When he released her breast, he squinted at her.

"They'll be a lot of changes, a lot to get used to for all of us. We don't need the negativity, the haters." He kissed her on the mouth and then along her neck. He started to undo her pants as he sought out her breast again with his mouth.

It felt so good and so right. Her uncle was wrong. Maybe he was even jealous at her success and his failures. She didn't know, but she was sure she loved Giuseppe, Andreas, and Dominick. She would try her best to respect their wishes and their commands. She just hoped they respected hers.

* * * *

Giuseppe didn't want to tell Giada about what had happened tonight. They all decided it was better for her to not really know their business and the dangers they were surrounded by. This deal with their friends' families was a profitable one but was off to a rough start. Nothing worthwhile ever came easy. His concern, as well as Dominick's and Andreas's, was Calvarro's interest in Giada still and the fact that one of his men was at her apartment in an SUV monitoring the place. He felt tense, and the only thing that would calm him and make him feel as though Giada was safe was having her close—this close. He stroked her nipple and slid his fingers into her pants.

"Lift for me. Show me you need my touch."

She was feminine, sexy, and he could crush her with his body. He felt masculine, as though he needed to bang on his chest and howl, indicating that he was the man, that she was his woman, and that if anyone tried to touch her they would suffer, if not die.

He slid his fingers lower as she lifted her hips and pushed her pants down. She looked away from him. "Will someone come in and see?"

"Maybe." He pressed his lips to hers. He slid his fingers into her cunt. He knew no one but his brother and his cousin would come back in. Brew could read his facial expression and knew that he would make love to Giada. None of the guards would dare enter now. The guards hadn't even wanted to join them for dinner, but Giada had been insistent that they stay.

Her lips parted as he released them and shoved two fingers into her cunt, thrusting faster, deeper.

"Giuseppe." She whispered his name, and his cock hardened.

"I need, Giada." He lifted, moved his fingers, and pulled down her pants and panties. He tossed them to the side and then turned her as he lowered to his knees on the rug, spread her thighs, and feasted on her cunt. She gripped his hair, and he lifted up.

"Arms above your head. Grab onto the couch and spread wide for me. Offer me every part of you," he ordered.

She complied, wide-eyed, shaking, but she complied. It drove his macho meter up a few notches, and he licked her from cunt to anus. Back and forth, on every swipe over her puckered hole, she moaned deeper.

"Giuseppe, I need, too."

He lifted, pushed down his pants, stepped from them, and then lowered again. He pulled her ass and cunt off the edge of the couch and went down on her again. He licked and thrust his fingers, exploring her cunt and her ass at the same time. She was wiggling and moaning.

"Where do you want my cock, baby? Where?" he asked, stroking his fingers into both holes.

"Everywhere. Everywhere." She gasped as she came.

He slid his fingers over her anus and pressed the cream in, lubricating it. He spread her wider. "Finger yourself. Feel how wet you are, how giving."

She looked shocked. He loved how inexperienced she was and how naughty he was going to make her with them. She was a natural submissive, but something told Giuseppe that Giada had a wild side. He gripped her hand, which wasn't lowering fast enough to her cunt. He speared a finger into her cunt as he pushed his cock into her ass. She gasped and began to try and close her legs.

"No. You've got this. You want it, baby. You're so turned on, and I need you like this. Giving, accepting." He slid the rest of the way in. Her fingers pushed into her cunt at the same time, and her lips parted.

"You're so naughty, Giuseppe. This is so naughty."

"Fuck yeah," he said through clenched teeth as he pulled a little bit out and then thrust deeper into her.

"Oh. Oh!" She got louder.

"Mine." He stroked into her faster and faster. She looked incredible, fingering her own pussy, those sexy, toned thighs wide and over his forearms and his dick disappearing into her ass. Her breasts moved side to side and up and down. He thrust his pelvis and rocked into her. "I love you, Giada. Know that I love you and that I never told a woman that before. Just you. Only you."

Her eyes glazed over, and she clenched her teeth and then exploded. He lost it in that moment and thrust again and again into her ass until he couldn't hold back any longer and came. He eased out of her ass and lifted her up into his arms. He lay over her on the couch, his bare ass facing the other way as he sucked on her neck and her breasts.

"I love you, too, Giuseppe. This is wild. I can't seem to get enough of each of you." She ran her fingers through his hair and over his shoulder.

Chapter 10

"I don't like it," Dominick stated firmly.

He stood in Giada's apartment with his hands on his hips, his gun in plain view, and a scowl on his face.

Dressed for work, Giada was a foot away from him. "I cannot—and will not—have guards around me while I am working. It isn't logical or needed. I'm at the workplace and in public places, and I thought you said that you don't really have any enemies, that you don't need guards like Fedarro and Mateus and the others do. I don't get it. Did you lie to me, Dominick?"

"I didn't lie to you. I'm concerned about Calvarro and Alajandro and Toro, never mind that uncle of yours who keeps calling."

She exhaled. "I know I'm not supposed to know what is going on with your business and all, but it's obvious you're under extra pressure. Don't add more by being ridiculous. This can't work if I have to have security with me. It can't. I'm going to get fired."

"If you get fired, then we'll take care of you completely," Giuseppe stated very seriously.

She threw up her hands. Then she went to grab her briefcase and purse, and as she bent over, Andreas wrapped an arm around her waist and hoisted her back up. He turned her around, had a palm over her ass, and stared down into her eyes.

"We need to work on these outfits for work. This is too damn sexy." He squeezed her ass.

She huffed and pouted. "This isn't fair. I didn't sign on for this, and it is unacceptable." She crossed her arms in front of her chest, and he smirked.

They were silent, and Train and Brew stood there, too, surrounding her in the center of the small kitchen. She was intimidated. Dominick looked at them and back at her.

"I know the head of security there. I can have her watched and the place monitored accordingly," Train stated.

"See, now he can have strange men in security booths behind closed doors looking at me through surveillance cameras as I adjust my breasts in my bra, lift my skirt to fix my thigh-high stockings, or—"

Andreas smacked her on the ass.

"Ouch!"

"Do you want to go to work without an escort for the day or not?" he asked her.

Brew chuckled.

"We'll work it out. It will be set before she arrives," Train said to them.

"Good. Now, wait for her outside. We have some rules to enforce before she leaves," Dominick said.

Train and Brew laughed then headed out of her apartment. Once the door closed, Dominick stared at her.

"You have a lot to learn about who is in charge and what type of men you belong to. I don't expect any more shit from you, Giada. This is serious stuff. We have things going on with work. People who are pissed and a bit of back-and-forth tit-for-tat crap we're trying to avoid turning into a nightmare of shit. So we would appreciate it if you would learn the rules quickly and abide by those rules. In fact, call Bella, Caprice, even Adelina and Gisella. Get their feedback and learn quickly, or you'll be spending a lot of time over our knees with our hands spanking that ass. That will be just the beginning of the punishments for disobedience."

She gulped.

"Get over there and kiss him good-bye," Giuseppe ordered.

She immediately went to Dominick, stood on her tiptoes, and kissed him as she slid her hands along his shoulders. He kissed her tenderly and ran his hands over her back and then to her ass. When he released her lips, he still looked angry as he turned and walked toward the door. Giuseppe kissed her next and then Andreas before she grabbed her things and they headed out the door.

"We'll have the guys bring you here after work to pack some clothes and things. You're staying with us," Dominick told her as they walked into the elevator along with Brew and Train.

"Wait, you want me to move in with you?" she asked.

They looked at her, and she swallowed hard and looked at Brew's and Train's backs.

"You aren't staying here alone," Giuseppe said to her.

"Um, isn't that moving things along kind of fast? I mean what if it's too much too soon and we get on one another's nerves, or I do something like act too clingy or needy or something like you're not used to, having a woman living in your place? It could be disastrous and—"

Giuseppe cupped her cheeks, and she stopped rambling.

"Giada, we want you with us. We've never asked a woman to live in our penthouse."

"We never had a woman sleep over or even be invited into our penthouse," Andreas added.

"I don't believe you," she said.

"Brew, Train?" Dominick said, and they turned to look at her.

"Never. No other women. Only you have ever been invited in or stayed the night," Brew told her.

She felt foolish.

"See? Now Brew and Train will come get you after work because we'll be tied up in a meeting, and then you'll come back here, pack some bags of clothes for a few days, and then meet us at our penthouse. We'll work out the week's schedule." Giuseppe kissed her.

The elevator doors opened, and they all headed out to the SUVs. She said good-bye one more time and then got into the SUV with Train and Brew. She fixed her lip gloss and looked at her flushed cheeks. Her life was really changing. She was going to have a bodyguard, escorts, and service to and from work and wherever.

"So I guess this means no more subways, busses, or taxis to work?" she asked.

Train smiled. "They're good men, Giada. They care about you and want to protect you. Trust them, and us, to do just that."

She gave a soft smile. "I'll try, Train, I really will, but I'm not used to this, not used to being cared for and taken care of. I just don't know how to give up that power of control."

"Something tells me that your men will teach you," Brew said.

"Very funny, Brew." She chuckled.

She wasn't sure how she was going to do this, but she prayed that she didn't get fired and that Alajandro and Toro hadn't complained to her bosses. No phone calls yet. Everything must be fine.

* * * *

"What do you want to do? They asked for a meeting to resolve any issues. The Fiorres are pissed off. Who the fuck took potshots at Roman and Sunny?" Louis Bronnos asked Calvarro.

"The fuck if I know. It wasn't me. I should owe one to whoever did take potshots and nearly killed Felix, that double-crossing snitch. Plus. whoever did it at least put a nice scare into Sunny Costanza and the Fiorres' main guy, Roman. They did set one of my biggest warehouses on fire. This shit needs to stop."

"Then negotiating with them is key."

"I don't know. It could be a setup," Calvarro said.

"Well, they believe it was you. They want to meet. Tonight, five o'clock at Club X. We can straighten shit out. Make a deal. Everyone we thought would back us up is out," Loppo added.

"What?"

"Yeah, fucking Andreas and a couple of his guys went and spoke with the connections. They even got in with the managers of all Alajandro and Toro's businesses. It's a done deal, Calvarro—a done deal. Let's get our cut. They might offer more than twenty percent," Louis Bronnos stated.

"Twenty percent? On our fucking industry? Our shit?" he yelled.

"We either cooperate or get taken out completely," Loppo said.

"Fucking bullshit. Bullshit!" Calvarro roared in anger and then paced. His cell phone rang, and he looked down, not recognizing the number. "Hello?"

"Calvarro Torres, this is your lucky day, and boy, do I have a deal for you."

* * * *

"Okay, I know you can't talk so we'll gather everyone up to meet tonight to discuss it. You must be going out of your mind," Gisella said over the phone.

"Oh God, it's crazy, Gisella. Absolutely crazy."

"I know, believe me. So I think the guys have some sort of meeting at Club X. Why don't we all meet there, have dinner and drinks, and help fill you in on rules and stuff," Gisella said.

"Oh, I'm supposed to go straight to my apartment and pack some clothes. They're insisting I stay with them."

"Of course they are. They'll be all male dominant and want to keep making love to you and have you close by. It strengthens the connection and also gives them a little peace of mind to see that you're okay and in eyesight. You'll get used to it."

"I don't know, Gisella. It's too soon. It was just the weekend really, Saturday and Sunday."

"After engaging in a ménage with those three, older, dominant, sexy men, are you tell me you'd rather sleep all alone in bed in your apartment?" Gisella asked her.

Giada exhaled.

"Didn't think so. Call your men and let them know the plan."

"Oh, I shouldn't."

"Well then I'll make sure the others know, and my men call yours to tell them the plans. By the time your security comes to pick you up, they'll know what's going on."

"Okay. Thanks so much for gathering everyone. I'm going crazy. I'm worried about my job, staying in this career, and dodging guys flirting with me in the office. I swear I think Train and Brew have the security here using the security cameras to watch my every move."

Gisella laughed. "They can't do that, but I'm certain any cameras that can check up on you will be. They want you safe, Giada, and after how those men were at the boxing event and at the club, I'd say your men have just cause to be cautious and protective of you. Never mind that video all over YouTube of you strutting that ass."

"Thanks for reminding me."

"All good when you're single. Not so good when you're not."

Giada chuckled. "See you tonight."

As she disconnected the call, she exhaled and then heard the knock on her door. Her boss, Monterro, was there.

"What's going on with you Alajandro and Toro?"

"What do you mean?" she asked.

"I mean they were supposed to send over the final contracts and they haven't yet." He looked at his watch. "It's nearly five already."

"I don't know why they haven't, and that really isn't my responsibility. It's billing's. You asked Margaret to confirm everything."

"I get the feeling these men want you to contact them, perhaps meet them and get those contracts in person."

"I can't."

"What do you mean you can't?"

"I have plans tonight."

"Well then tomorrow for lunch or something. They like you."

"It's business and nothing more. I'm seeing someone."

He squinted at her. "Since when?

"It's new, Monterro. I'll call Alajandro myself and find out if he can have them dropped off."

"Or you can pick them up in person. Come on, Giada. You landed this contract and negotiated the terms. This is a big account."

"Okay."

He nodded with that stern expression before leaving her office. She took a few unsteady breaths. Should she call Dominick and tell him? *Jesus, why the hell would I do that? This is business and nothing more.*

She took out her cell and made the call.

"Hello, Giada. So nice to hear from you," Alajandro said to her.

He sounded okay. Maybe this wouldn't be so bad. "Hello, Alajandro. I was just checking in to make sure you're all set with the contracts. Monterro stopped in and was concerned because they weren't here and Margaret hadn't heard from you. Are there any questions or any assistance needed?"

"There may be. Perhaps you're available for dinner?"

"Oh, so sorry, but I have plans with my friends. If there's anything you don't understand in the contract, I can have Margaret give you a call, or she could stop by and collect the contracts at your office."

"Toro and I would prefer seeing you."

She swallowed hard. "Well, I don't think that's really necessary."

"It is necessary if you want this deal to go through. What about right now?" he asked.

"It's nearly five."

"I understand that. On your way to wherever you're going you could stop in at Carlitto's, and we could sign the documents electronically. Do you know where that is?"

"I know where it is, but—"

"No *but*s, Giada. Show up at five, and we'll sign them. Have a drink with us to seal the deal, and then you can meet your friends."

She thought about her boss, Monterro, and his concerns about sealing this deal. It had been her doing from the start so she had to finish it. She would then make sure that someone else from the company would take on the responsibility of checking the accounts and getting approval from his security team.

"Okay, I'll meet you for the contracts at five."

"A drink, too, to celebrate," he added.

"Okay, Alajandro. Five o'clock."

She ended the call and immediately felt uneasy. She rubbed her palms down the skirt of her dress. It was very tight and sort of sexy without the light sweater, but she knew she was going to Club X after work to meet the girls and then the guys after they had their meeting. She should call them and tell them about this meeting with Alajandro. She looked at her watch. She'd spoken to Giuseppe earlier, and he'd said that they were unavailable from four thirty until after the meeting and that they would catch up with her at the club. She couldn't disturb them in this meeting. It sounded serious.

She stood and gathered her things. There was a knock at the door to her office.

"Giada, there is some superhot guy waiting for you in the waiting area. He said he's your escort." Julia raised her eyebrows in question.

She knew immediately it was Brew. She smiled. "That's probably Brew. I'll be out momentarily. I just need to grab my things. Can you also let Monterro know that I'm meeting Alajandro and Toro to sign the contracts? I'll send them right to him and Margaret to finalize."

"Meeting them? But you have a personal escort. Is Brew one of their security guys?" Julia asked.

"No. Brew works for the Coglonie family."

Julia covered her mouth, closed the office door, and looked at her.

"Are you serious? Aren't they the owners of Club X and like a bunch of other bars and clubs across the city? They're superhot, and dangerous, too."

"They're actually pretty nice guys, but yes, they own a lot of businesses, and they are very attractive."

"Oh my God, Giada. I hope you're not getting romantically involved with those men. They have very bad reputations, especially with women. I've heard things."

"What things?" Giada asked, suddenly feeling unsure, which was stupid. People gossiped all the time.

"My friends and I go to several clubs, including Club X, and I've seen them with women hanging on their arms or their tongues down their throats. They can basically get any woman they want, and they do. They're not the commitment types at all. In fact, my friend Leslie, who can be a bit wild, she kind of fooled around with the one guy who is super-serious."

Giada didn't want to believe this. She figured her friend was lying or maybe exaggerating the truth.

"He had scars on his chest. Like knife and bullet wounds Leslie thought."

Giada felt sick. "When was this? Like a long time ago?"

Julia shook her head slowly. She then made a face as though she was sorry to tell her.

"When?" Giada asked, raising her voice slightly.

"A week ago or so."

Giada's eyes widened.

"This little fooling-around session happened at the club?"

"In one of the special rooms they have upstairs that overlook the dance floor. She said he was wild, took her from behind after she saw his scars and gasped. He got pissed and was super-rough with her, but when he was done, Leslie said he had this look in his eyes like he wasn't himself. Scary, like the man wasn't with it. He lied about taking her home to his penthouse and sharing her with two guys. Leslie totally wanted to try the ménage, but then it didn't happen."

Giada felt sick to her stomach, and it only got worse.

"I'm sorry to tell you this if you thought they were nice guys. If it's the big guy with the muscles you did whatever with, just know he can't be trusted. Those kinds of men just pretend to care and want to own you, put a guard on you to make you think you're important to them, but they just want to have sex with you whenever they can."

Giada looked at Julia and straightened out her shoulders. "I can't believe it."

"I'm so sorry. If I had known you even liked them or knew them, I would have told you sooner."

"No. Of course you didn't know. Things just happened this weekend." She thought about her emotions, about going to Jimmy's gravesite, and about being in love with Andreas, Giuseppe, and Dominick. Were they lying to her? Using her?

"Hey, why don't you ask them about it? Ask him about Leslie and making out with her in the hallway by the bar and then taking her upstairs. If he says anything like he didn't make out with her or she was throwing herself at him, then you'll know he's lying."

She looked at her phone. "I need to go. I have to meet Alajandro and Toro at Carlitto's."

"Oh, okay. I'm really sorry, Giada. Really," Julia told her, and Julia had tears in her eyes.

Giada felt numb. She touched her secretary's arm and gave a soft smile. "I appreciate the truth and you not hiding it from me."

"Never, Giada. I wouldn't make you look like a fool like that Coglonie guy is doing. Maybe you should stay away from Club X and also get rid of that Brew guy."

She nodded and headed out to the waiting room. One look at Brew and she saw his facial expression change from a small smile to a scowl. He looked past her at Julia, then placed his hand against her back, and escorted her to the elevator. Giada saw some of the other staff watching. It made her feel like a whore, like some used goods, a woman being entertained by made men for the time being. Her heart ached as the elevator doors closed. *Could it be true?*

"Giada, what's wrong?"

"Nothing."

"Bullshit nothing. I can tell something is wrong."

"I don't really want to talk about it, Brew."

He exhaled, then the doors opened, and they came out to the main lobby of the large upscale office building and bank. He escorted her along the way, and she felt uneasy, as though eyes were on her, watching her, like people were laughing at her, and she wanted to cry. She couldn't, though. She had to get through meeting with Alajandro and Toro.

"We need to make a stop at Carlitto's. You know where that is?" she asked Train as they got into the SUV.

"Carlitto's? Why? I thought we were going to your apartment for clothes and then to Club X to meet your friends," Train said from the front driver's seat.

"I have to meet a client and get documents electronically signed."

"What client?" Brew asked and looked at his cell phone.

"Alajandro and Toro," she said as Train pulled into traffic.

"What?" Brew asked.

"I need to. The contracts haven't been sent, and I called him earlier. He wants me present to sign the documents electronically and then send them to my boss, who is waiting on them, and then celebrate with a drink. I don't have a choice, Brew."

"We can't call the bosses," Train said to him.

"No, they're in a meeting, I know that. It won't be a situation. It won't take too long because they know I have plans with friends."

"They aren't trustworthy, and their cousin Calvarro is one of the men meeting with your men as we speak."

She swallowed hard. "I don't need to know that. Your bosses don't tell me anything or want me to know anything. I get it, Brew,

Train. Now please just take me to this meeting so I can be done with this. Then I'll decide if I'm going to Club X or not."

"What do you mean going to Club X or not?" Train asked her.

She exhaled and leaned back, looking out the window. Tears filled her eyes. She felt used, yet her gut clenched at the idea that Andreas was the man Leslie had sex with. But she knew about the scars on his chest. Could it be true and only happened last week? A tear fell, and she wiped it away.

"Giada?"

When Brew said her name, she shook her head. "I can't talk about it."

Her cell phone buzzed. She looked at it grateful for the distraction as Bella texted that they would all meet by six at Club X. She couldn't help but wonder if Bella's men had cheated on her too? Had the others? Was it the way things were dating made men? She thought a ménage was supposed to be so special. She'd started to feel pretty angry, and by the time she got to Carlitto's, she was fighting the combination of emotions inside—jealousy, disappointment, hurt, anger—and she tempered it down.

"I'm going to remain nearby. I don't like this, and I know your men are going to be pissed off at this," Brew told her as they walked to the entrance of the busy bar. It was happy hour, and all the business people were blowing off steam from working all day.

"Do what you think is right. I'll do what is necessary to get this over with."

He squinted at her. "Something is wrong. I can tell. What is it, Giada?"

She shook her head. "I'm a big girl, Brew. I guess I'm learning what it's going to be like to be this week's lover of the Coglonie men."

His eyes narrowed, but then she heard her name. She put on a fake smile, and Alajandro and Toro greeted her with kisses to her cheek hello and annoyed looks at Brew.

"What's he doing here?" Toro asked her.

"The Coglonie men assigned him to me. I'm seeing them now. I'm sure you know. Let's go do this," she stated firmly and saw Brew looking at them with anger, but Alajandro didn't seem affected as he placed a hand at her lower back and took her over to the high bar stools and table in the corner. Brew had to remain a good distance away because of the crowds of people.

They sat, and she crossed her legs and pulled out her small iPad that the contracts could be signed on. Toro covered her hand.

"First things first." He stared at her mouth.

She thought he was going to kiss her, but then he squinted at her.

"Something is wrong."

She looked down. "What?" she asked and then looked at Alajandro, who glanced toward where Brew was and then back at her.

"You aren't really getting involved with those Coglonie men, are you? I mean you know they aren't serious about you?" Toro asked.

Alajandro placed his hand on the back of her chair and caressed her shoulder, but obviously Brew couldn't see, or he would be over here tearing the guy's arm off.

She opened her iPad. "Let's sign these and then have that drink. I could use it."

Alajandro smiled, and then they looked over the documents, and both men signed them. Toro ran his hand along her knee under the table while Alajandro caressed her back. She moved her leg.

"Don't, Toro. There can never be anything between the three of us." She placed her iPad back into her bag after she forwarded the contracts to Monterro and Margaret.

Toro clicked his fingers, and the waiter came over with a bottle of Patrón and three glasses. He poured them, and then Alajandro made the toast. "To us and doing business together, plus pleasure," he said, and they clinked glasses.

"Minus the pleasure part," she said and downed the Patrón, letting the burning sensation smooth over the turmoil boiling in her gut.

"You look amazing and very sexy in this dress. I bet you're wearing something extra sexy underneath there," Toro said and stroked her thigh.

She pushed his hand off her. "Toro, what did I say?"

Alajandro slid his hand under her hair to her neck and squeezed. She gasped.

"We had you all wrong, Giada. Thought you were all sweet, shy, and inexperienced. If we knew you liked cock in every hole, we would have taken you that night at your apartment and shown you how good both of us are in bed. Those three assholes can't compare," Toro said to her and squeezed her thigh.

She went to move, and he gripped her upper arm tight and turned sideways so Brew couldn't see what he was doing.

"They're using you. We don't mind, though. You've got a hot body, and now that you've fucked three men, no man will ever see you as anything but a whore."

His words struck her hard. She wanted to cry, but something snapped inside of her, her anger with the Coglonie men, her disappointment, and her jealousy. She slid her hand to his crotch, and his hold on her arm, which surely would leave bruising, lightened. She stroked his cock and gave him a smile.

"You're so right, Toro," she said.

Alajandro snickered. "Jesus, she's a fucking piece of work. I told you it was an act." He leaned down and kissed her neck.

That was when she made her move.

She gripped Toro's crotch tight, and he yelled out, slammed her hand away from his crotch, grabbed her face, and kissed her. She heard the yelling, the sound of the table falling over and Alajandro grunt as she used her martial arts moves on Toro. A knee to his crotch had him pulling her close to him, and she countered his move with another kick. As he stepped back recovering and went to strike her, she punched him straight in the jaw. He fell backward onto his ass, and the place roared with commotion. Brew grabbed her and pulled her along as everyone in the bar laughed at Toro and Alajandro.

"What the fuck. The bosses are going to flip out. Jesus, Giada."

"God that felt so good. Those two jerks had the nerve to say the things they did to me. Assholes!" she blurted out.

He pulled opened the door to the SUV, and they both got into the back.

"What's going on?"

"Get the hell out of here fast," Brew told Train.

Then Brew tossed her bags onto the seat. She stretched her hand out, and tears rolled down her cheeks. She was shaking. Brew took her hand, and he turned toward her.

"Fuck. It's swelling up good. And your lipstick is smeared, your lip's swollen, and shit, and your fucking arm. I should have gotten to you sooner."

"No, Brew. They planned that."

"What the fuck happened?" Train asked as he drove.

Brew explained. "We can get ice on that hand. You can fix up at your apartment."

"No. It's late. Just go to the club so I can meet my friends."

Brew touched her cheek and had his palm against it. He stared down into her eyes. "Your men are going to be fucking pissed."

"We took care of it together, Brew. It's over."

"No, it isn't over. Those two guys are going to suffer serious consequences for what they did to you, the woman of the Coglonie men."

"I wouldn't jump the gun yet, Brew. Perhaps I'm not as important as you think." She turned away and held her hand to her chest.

"What is that supposed to mean?" Train asked before Brew could.

"It means I know what I am to them. I get it, so let's not sugarcoat it please. Just go to the club. I won't need clothes from my apartment. I'm staying in my apartment tonight—alone."

Brew exhaled, and she didn't answer his questions or respond to him. She just stared out the window; felt her fingers and hand throbbing; absorbed the pain there and on her arm, which was surely bruised; and welcomed it. Her heart ached with sadness. Could this all be a game? A temporary sexual fling leaving her as used goods so that men like Toro and Alajandro would be the kind of men she'd have to deal with for the rest of her life?

She felt hollow inside, and the tears rolled down her cheeks, but she wiped them away. She had to be strong. She was going to see her friends and talk to them. Could they be trusted, or would Bella, Caprice, Gisella, and the others tell her that this was life involved with made men? That they could have sex with other women, order them around, and isolate them from everything except what those made men wanted their women to know about? Anger pooled in her belly once more. She wished she were a little taller and had a longer reach. Then her punch would have broken Toro's nose. He wouldn't be so good-looking for a while. That was for sure. She clenched her teeth. What was she going to do?

* * * *

Calvarro stared at Fedarro as they gathered in the meeting room. The atmosphere was tense, to say the least. Giuseppe, Andreas, and Dominick were remaining straight-faced and not giving up any emotions to read, but Calvarro knew they were pissed. They didn't have a clue as to what was coming their way.

"So we have an understanding and agreement of terms?" Fedarro said to Calvarro as they all sat around the meeting room upstairs at Club X.

Calvarro looked at all of them, at Sunny, Vinny, Dominick, Andreas, Giuseppe, Mateus, and Major.

"We know when it's smarter to back down, Fedarro, although the thirty percent is kind of slim considering this was our business we started," Calvarro said, feeling anger pool in his belly. He hoped that man came through on his promise. It was killing him inside to back down to these fucking men.

"You need to understand that multiple large families are involved with this operation. We can give a certain amount to ease the pain of your loss, but this isn't your market. Anyone with connections in Cuba can make these imports happen. We have the power, the resources, and the security to do it right and efficiently. You get to keep control through the small businesses your cousins have established. That's fair," Fedarro said to him.

"Not really, but as you say, there are multiple families involved here, so we'll accept the thirty percent cut." Calvarro felt the bile rise in his throat. He couldn't believe he was accepting this. The end result would be Dominick and Giuseppe dead, so it would be worth it in the end.

Fedarro stuck out his hand. Calvarro shook it.

"Join us for a drink?" Fedarro asked.

Calvarro eyed over Dominick and Giuseppe. "Only if Giada is joining us. That's one woman I'll never get enough of looking at. So sweet and some dancer, too. When is Latin night at your place, Morano? I want to see Giada move that body in person."

Loppo smirked. The other men all had scowls on their faces.

"I think it's time for you to leave," Andreas stated firmly.

Calvarro smirked. "We'll be in touch."

Royce and Logic, two of the security guys for the Coglonie men, walked them out. As they headed downstairs, Calvarro caught sight of Giada and her friends leaving the dining area. Her hand was wrapped, and Loppo whispered to him.

"Toro and Alajandro succeeded in their plan, but it seems Giada has some martial arts skills after all."

"Really?" he asked, feeling surprised. She was so petite. He thought the classes she took were for exercise, not technique.

"We'll need to keep that in mind for future reference."

"Exactly," Loppo added.

* * * *

"That fucking piece of shit. We don't need him. We should just take him out completely," Giuseppe stated once Calvarro left the room.

"He's a dick. We know that, and he was just trying to get under your skin," Fedarro said.

"It worked because he got under mine. I understand you're upset guys but just remember that Giada is yours and she's here, safe and sound," Morano stated. Then someone knocked on the door. Vinny opened it, and Train and Brew entered, looking grim.

"Logic and Royce are watching over Giada. There was a situation earlier," Train told them.

"What situation?" Dominick asked, feeling pissed off.

"We knew you were in this meeting, so we had to handle it accordingly, and things got out of hand," Brew said.

"What happened?" Giuseppe asked.

Brew explained and then told them what Alajandro and Toro had done and then what he and Giada had done. Dominick was pissed off.

"Where is she now? Is her hand okay? The bruising?" Giuseppe asked as Andreas began to head toward the door.

"Wait, Andreas," Train said.

Dominick felt his chest tightened.

"Something happened prior to us leaving her office. We don't know what, but she was really upset—sad, hurt—and she wouldn't tell us a thing. Then she looked angry, and I guess when those two assholes made their moves, that anger came out fast. She made some comments about not staying with you guys tonight and staying at her place alone. Just so you know. Something isn't right," Brew told them.

"Damn, what the fuck do you want to do about this?" Fedarro asked.

"What should we do? Put a full beating on those two assholes and make it known not to fuck with us?" Giuseppe said.

"Something will have to be done, but not now when the three of you are as furious as you are. You need to talk to Giada. Comfort her, make sure that she's okay, and find out what happened. Despite Calvarro shaking our hands and saying he was accepting the deal, I don't believe him or trust him. Alajandro and Toro are his cousins, his family. Something isn't adding up, and we all need to be on guard— you three especially with Giada. Calvarro knows she's special to each of you. It could be some sort of trap," Fedarro told them.

"I agree completely," Dominick stated as anger pooled in his belly. The need to see Giada and hold her, comfort her, filled him, yet he held back, not knowing how he would react to seeing her and the bruises.

He looked at Giuseppe and Andreas. "Make sure that she's okay. I'll be down momentarily." Dominick looked at Fedarro and Mateus.

The others left the room, leaving just the three of them, Dominick, Mateus, and Fedarro.

"Did you get that client list of Giada's?" Dominick asked.

"We did, Dominick, and I have to say, your suspicions aren't justified. She's a good woman. She's sweet, caring, and she isn't some sort of plant or trick to destroy you guys and your operations."

"Fedarro, you know I have enemies who will go to great lengths to destroy me. They may not have struck in years, but that doesn't mean they aren't out there waiting, planning to strike. Giuseppe and I always trust our instincts and act on them accordingly. I had to be sure."

"Understood. No names or clients of concern came up. She's done very well in that company she works for. We took additional steps to ensure we investigated accordingly. We even looked at her secretary, Julia," Mateus said.

"And?"

"She is a little shady. Hangs out at Cha Cha Cabana a lot."

"Any connection to Calvarro or his cousin?"

"Not that we found, but to ease any concern, we put a guy on her. If she goes there, he'll know who she is in contact with and get back to us," Mateus said to him.

Dominick nodded.

"Dominick, it's obvious you three love her. Whatever is going on, whatever fears you have, face them and be honest with her. We understand what it feels like, the weakness that forms. Don't leave her exposed to danger again. Keep her close because, as we all have learned, enemies will go to great lengths to put a knife through our hearts and make us suffer. Going after the women we love is open game for them," Fedarro told him.

Dominick nodded. "I will need to deal with Alajandro and Toro accordingly to send a clear message."

"Understood. We'll assist. Mateus is good at causing pain and getting points across." Fedarro chuckled.

"I'm pretty damn good at that, too," Dominick said.

They smiled.

"I say put Andreas on it but be sure he doesn't kill them. We don't need any cops sniffing around the operation," Mateus said.

They all laughed. Andreas was a wild one. He did what he wanted when he wanted. He was an enforcer, the head of security, and more. When it came to women, he didn't do commitments, just took what he wanted and needed, as women threw themselves at him. He was different with Giada.

This was real. It meant more, and they needed to get used to this commitment and helping her to understand what her position was as their woman and about the decisions she made. She never should have been at that bar meeting those men. He would make her understand the mistakes she'd made and help her to realize the different mind-set she needed to have.

* * * *

Giada had the girls laughing. The guys' meeting was taking longer than anticipated, and as they were all talking about life being involved with made men and about what had happened to Giada, they drank. By the time their men joined them, all the women were feeling pretty tipsy, Giada included.

"I can't believe that you grabbed him by the balls," Caprice said loudly.

"No, no, she stroked him first to make him loosen his hold on her inner thigh," Bella added.

They all laughed.

"Holy crap, Giada. You are filled with surprises," Gisella said.

They laughed loudly.

Royce and the other guards were all nearby and in earshot of the conversation, but none of them cared. Giada saw Andreas and Giuseppe approach and then Royce whisper to them, and their expressions hardened even more. Giuseppe came up next to her.

"Hey, what the hell happened tonight?" he asked her, placing his hands on her shoulders.

"She kicked ass is what happened," Caprice said.

They all started hooting and hollering. Giada smiled and lowered her eyes to her hand. It was red and swollen. She still felt it. "Another shot."

They cheered some more.

"Maybe you need to slow down," Andreas stated with his arms crossed in front of his chest.

She made a sound and waved her hand at him. "Nah, I can still feel the pain." She lifted her hand for Giuseppe to see.

Giuseppe looked at it. "Shit. Have you been icing it?"

She leaned back and showed him how the material on her dress was wet. "Yes! And look at this—a wet dress." She slammed her good hand down on the table, and the others laughed and told her it was okay and it was just water. Then the other men joined their women, and they looked amused, to say the least. Giada wasn't drunk, but a few more drinks and some shots and she would be. It didn't numb the pain in her heart either.

"We need to talk, baby. Come with me," Giuseppe said to her.

"No." She pushed his hand off her shoulder.

"Giada," Andreas said her name loudly.

She stared up at him with all those muscles and that hard, fierce expression. She didn't feel intimidated. She felt angry. Tears stung her eyes, and he narrowed his eyes at her.

"Come with us now," he ordered.

Bella gave her leg a tap. "They look upset. Go with them," she whispered.

Giada squinted. She thought about what Julia had said, about Leslie. She stood and teetered slightly, but then Giuseppe placed his hands on her hips and guided her. She hated that it felt so good, that his touch eased her upset and the fear she had tonight at Carlitto's and having to defend herself.

As they passed Andreas, he joined them and walked with them. "Where are you taking me?" she asked as they got into the hallway and toward the elevators.

"Upstairs to one of the booths," Andreas said and stroked her hair.

When they got into the elevator, she stared up at him with anger in her eyes. "So it's like that then? I'm like the others, Andreas?"

He squinted at her. "What?"

She turned away from him as the elevator doors opened, and there stood Fedarro, Mateus, and Dominick.

"So they're all in on it? Mateus and Fedarro, too?" she asked.

"All in on what?" Giuseppe asked.

"The women you take up here, the ones you hook up with downstairs then bring up here and screw. Then you're done with them and dismiss them like crap."

She walked past them. Andreas grabbed her arm.

"What are you talking about?"

"The women, damn you. I heard all about it today. Before I left to meet Alajandro and Toro, I was told about the woman, Leslie, you just hooked up with up here last week. I know about the women, and that you three don't take this seriously, that I'm just another woman to screw around with, okay?" She raised her voice, and the tears fell.

"That's a lie," Andreas said to her.

She looked at all of them. "How could you? How could all of you do things like that when your women love you and adore you?"

"Giada, who told you these things?" Fedarro asked her.

She stared at him. She knew he was powerful. More so than her men she assumed.

"Answer him," Dominick scolded.

"Julia told me all about her friend Leslie and Andreas and about how all of you cheat on your women you claim are solely yours and that you're faithful to."

"Lies. They're lies," Andreas said, scolding her.

"Mateus," Dominick said to him, and he looked at Fedarro.

"We're on it. Take care of her and make her understand," Fedarro said, and he and Mateus walked into the elevator and left.

Andreas grabbed her arm where the bruising was. She gasped and pulled back as he released her, realizing it hurt.

"I'm bruised there from Toro's hold."

They entered the room, a private area that overlooked the dance floor below.

"Sit down," Dominick demanded.

"No. I'm done taking orders from you. I'm not going to be used. Men like Toro and Alajandro will continue to harass me now that they know I've been with three men. You've ruined me, and it was done on purpose to make me be obedient and loyal to each of you. I get it."

Andreas gripped her waist and pulled her closer to him. "You don't get it. Lies, Giada, lies spread to make you distrust us. I did not have sex with any women here last week. I haven't been with any women for months, Giada—months."

She let the tear escape her eyes. "I don't know what to believe."

Dominick spoke. "Look at me. Now."

She turned with Andreas's assistance and his hands on her waist. She hated how good it felt, hated it right now.

"You're our woman. We're committed to you and only you. We've opened up our hearts to you, Giada, and we've never, ever done that before. That's the truth. Your secretary, Julia, lied," Dominick stated.

"No, no, it was her friend who had sex with you—that you, Andreas, took her up, bent her over and screwed her, then tossed her out. She knew you had scars on your chest. She knew," Giada yelled and pulled away from him. She crossed her arms in front of her chest and gasped as she hit her swollen hand.

"Andreas, the woman last week who came up to you all drunk. Remember? Royce had to pull her from you. She ripped your shirt opened," Giuseppe said to him.

"Fuck. It was a setup."

"Oh please. Who the hell does something like that? God, you really think I'm that stupid? That gullible?" she asked and wiped her eyes.

"No, baby, but these people, they're good at what they do, at wanting to tear us apart, put a wedge between us so we let down our guards, or you insist on being alone instead of with one of us and under our protection," Giuseppe stated.

"They are lies, Giada, and we'll get to the bottom of this with Julia and Leslie. Being with us means people will do what they can to destroy what we have, to break us down, and to make you distrust us. It's part of what you need to learn to deal with," Dominick said so coldly to her she was shocked.

"To deal with?"

"You're upset for multiple reasons. You've been drinking, you're hurt, and now is not the time to try to make you understand your place and position in our lives. Follow your gut, Giada. Did you forget how to do that?" Dominick said, challenging her.

She stared at him and listened to her gut. Were they lies? She hadn't wanted to believe them because she was in love with the Coglonie men. Was there a way to prove they were lies?

"Think about it. People will lie to make you distrust us. Alajandro and Toro lied about needing those contracts signed when they really wanted to make another play on you. Calvarro even made a comment upstairs in the meeting to piss us off. I don't trust Calvarro or his cousins and this woman Julia. We have men looking into her now, and we will find out what's going on. Did you know that Julia hangs out at Cha Cha Cabana?"

Her eyes widened.

"No, I didn't think so, and I'm sure you know who owns that place and his connections to Calvarro and his cousins," Dominick said.

Tears rolled down her cheeks. "They said things to me." She thought about how maybe Dominick, Andreas, and Giuseppe were telling the truth about people lying to put a wedge between them, how Julia had said the things she did, and then how Alajandro and Toro had said what they had about men thinking of her as a whore now that she'd screwed three men. She covered her belly with her hand.

"What did they say to you?" Dominick demanded to know.

She turned to look at them. "That now that I was with the three of you, had sex with three men, no other man will think of me as anything but a whore."

"I'm going to kill them," Andreas stated.

"No. There's more to this—a setup, something to make us take the bait and go after them. You saw Calvarro in the meeting. He wasn't really accepting the partnership, but it was like he was appeasing us for now, like he was going to get the last laugh," Dominick said.

"It could be anything, Dominick. We have enemies, people who would love to see us go under," Giuseppe stated.

"Or it could be just Calvarro wanting to cause trouble and give a fighting shot at surviving among the fittest," Dominick said and then stared at Giada.

"You need to accept our commands, our authority, and know that we love you and do what we do to protect you from men like this and women like Julia, who more than likely has been used. We'll prove that to you shortly. Now come here," he ordered.

She swallowed hard. She felt so confused, yet what they said made perfects sense. Her own mind whirled with investigating and finding out the truth. She would find out. She would get it from Julia, and she would handle it accordingly. She walked slowly toward Dominick.

He reached out, cupped her cheek, and brushed his thumb along her lips. "You're swollen here."

She didn't tell him it was because of the forceful way Toro had kissed her.

He took her hand and looked at the swelling. "We'll ice it more but know how proud I am of you defending yourself and using the tools you know to take back control. However, you never should have been there. Brew and Train should have called me or taken it upon themselves to order you not to go. They'll be dealt with accordingly."

"No, Dominick. It wasn't their fault. It was simply going to be a meeting to sign the contracts and then have a drink and leave, so it was all business. None of us knew it was a trap. Don't get angry with Brew and Train. They were there for me and got to me so quickly. They were very upset. Please, Dominick." She placed her palm against his chest.

He hoisted her closer and narrowed his eyes down at her. "You'll take their punishment for them?"

She felt aroused, needy. "Yes," she whispered.

"Hmm, well, we need to join the others back downstairs. That punishment will come later tonight when you're at the penthouse."

"Oh, I didn't go by the apartment and get any clothes," she said, and then Giuseppe's hands landed on her shoulders. She glanced up at him.

"You won't be needing any," he said, and then Dominick pressed closer and kissed her.

She hugged him, and when he released her lips, she pressed close and squeezed him tight. His hand slid along her ass and squeezed.

"You're going to have a very sore ass by the time we're done spanking you."

She pulled back. "A spanking?" she asked, feeling both shocked and aroused.

"Among other things." Giuseppe pulled her closer to him and kissed her.

He, too, ran his palm along her ass and then up her back to her hair. She tilted her chin up toward him.

"No using your martial arts on us, though. You accept your punishments, and we guarantee pleasure," Giuseppe stated and kissed her again.

Andreas pulled her by her hand over to the couch. He lifted her up and then placed her over his lap. "You two can wait until later. I'm going to give her a small sample of what's to come since it was me she thought was a male whore and used this room to fuck women."

"Andreas!" she screamed out just as his hand landed on her ass, hard.

He spanked her several times as his brothers laughed, and then he lifted her up into a cradle position on his lap, cupped her cheeks, and stared down into her eyes.

"I love you, woman. Never said those words to any other woman ever. Not even to get her to spread her thighs." He winked.

She gave his shoulder a smack. "That kind of teasing is going to cost you, Andreas."

"Oh really?" he asked and then began tickling her.

She held her swollen hand out of the way and laughed as he pulled her close and hugged her tight.

"Any time you want me to fuck you up here in this room I'll make an exception," he said, continuing to tease her.

"I don't think so, Andreas," she said to him, and he stood with her in his arms and placed her feet on the floor. She fixed her dress, and Giuseppe looked at her hand.

"We're icing this the second we get downstairs," he told her and kissed the top of her head.

"Okay, but shots help to ease the ache better," she said, walking into the hallway.

Brew, Train, and Logic were waiting there, and something told her they'd overheard the conversation in the room.

"I think you need to slow down on the shots. You get a little mouthy, Giada," Andreas said to her as they all got into the elevator.

"I guess that's why they call it liquid courage."

"Who needs that when you have a right hook like you do?" Brew said to her.

She chuckled.

"I'd rather not think about our woman having to use her fists and fight for herself when we should have been there to protect her, as should have our security," Dominick said very seriously.

She noticed that Brew and Train looked upset. "Sometimes it takes a woman decking a man and putting him in his place to make him see that not all women are weak, but can be capable. I don't think Brew decking Toro would have had the same effect that me doing it did. At least the crowd seemed to find it very amusing."

"There was a crowd watching and cheering after she decked him?" Logic asked, smiling.

"Oh, she made a hell of a scene. Probably would be there still and doing shots with her new fans if I didn't drag her out of there," Brew teased.

They laughed as the elevator doors opened.

"Never underestimate a woman and definitely not the sweet, quiet, petite ones," Logic said.

They all headed into the crowd and back over to their friends. A hand on her ass and one on her hip and she knew these men were going to give her reminders all night about what was to come once they had her alone and naked. Boy, was she looking forward to her first spanking ever by all her men.

She leaned into Dominick and pressed her face against his chest as they joined their friends, and as the night went on and his hand stilled at her waist, she eased it to her rear and looked up at him. Their gazes locked.

"I love you, Dominick. I'm sorry I thought the worse."

"I love you, too," he said and gave her rear a squeeze.

His hand remained on her for quite some time, and she didn't care one bit.

Chapter 11

"Dominick! Oh God!" She cried out as he thrust into her ass and smacked it at the same time. She couldn't take it any longer. Her ass cheeks burned from their first round of spankings, and now Andreas was deep inside of her cunt and Dominick was thrusting into her ass, spanking her some more. She was exhausted yet aroused for the fourth time already. Were they going to screw her all night long?

"Ready, baby?" Giuseppe said, gripping her hair and bringing her mouth to his cock.

He'd just gotten washed up after bending her over the couch in the living room and screwing her over the couch for the second time.

She licked her lips and accepted his cock as he leaned closer toward her mouth. She began to suck on it, and she convulsed from another orgasm. She was losing her ability to remain upright, and then she heard Dominick roar his release. He slowly pulled from her ass, and then Andreas was next.

"Fuck. I need more," Giuseppe stated and pulled her from his cock. He lifted her off Andreas and brought her to the edge of the bed. He placed her feet on the floor and got right in behind her to thrust into her pussy from behind.

"Oh, Giuseppe. I can't. I can hardly stand, and I won't be able to walk tomorrow."

"Good!" all three men said at once and snickered.

Smack.

Smack.

"Oh!" she cried out, and her pussy leaked more cream.

Giuseppe set a wild, fast pace as Andreas and Dominick got cleaned up. Her legs were shaking so much. She couldn't believe this. Their punishment was to make love to her so many times that she'd pass out? Her eyes glazed over. She was losing focus when she came again, and then Giuseppe followed, calling out her name and spanking her several more times. She fell to the bed. And he massaged her shoulders, her back, and then her ass. It stung. He kissed along her skin where his hands had gone, and when he got to her ass, he looked at it.

"What do you two think, pink enough?" he asked them.

Dominick and Andreas moved closer and ran their palms along the cheeks. She tightened up.

"No more, please. It's sensitive."

"Hey, don't forget that you're the one who kept asking for more, hell, begging to be spanked harder." Andreas leaned down to kiss her shoulder.

She turned to look at him, her cheeks warm. "Well, I liked it, but I think I asked for too much."

"It will be fine. Something tells me this won't be the last time we spank this ass,'" Andreas said and then gave it a tap.

"Oh." She exhaled and lifted.

"Shower, then bed," Dominick ordered.

She looked at the clock as Dominick lifted her up into his arms and carried her from their bedroom to the bathroom. It was after 3 a.m. "Oh God, I'm not going to be able to get up for work."

"You aren't going tomorrow. Work from here, and then we'll grab your clothes from your apartment. We need to talk about you moving in here with us."

"What?" she said to Dominick.

"We want you here with us every day and every night, Giada," Dominick told her.

Tears filled her eyes. "So soon? Are you sure?"

"Honey, we are not about to start doing the whole sleep-at-your-place-then-at-our-place thing. It makes no sense when we want you to be between us when we go to sleep at night and when we wake up in the morning."

She smiled at Giuseppe's words. "Really?"

"Yes. Now shower, then bed," Dominick said to her.

"Yes, sir, boss man."

He set her down in the shower.

Smack.

"Hey."

He narrowed his eyes in warning. "Watch it, wiseass, or you'll be doing a hell of a lot more standing than sitting."

Her cheeks blushed, but she heard Andreas and Giuseppe chuckle. She stepped under the hot water and moaned softly. Oh yeah, she was definitely going to be spanked a lot by these men, especially by Dominick.

* * * *

Dominick heard his phone ringing, saw that it was Mateus and answered it.

"What did you find out?" Dominick asked Mateus.

"This Julia woman was with that Leslie chick who came onto Andreas that night out of nowhere. They were hanging out having drinks with Apponte last night," Mateus told him.

"Calvarro's other guard. Fuck."

"I know. They were or are planning something. What is Giada going to do about work?" Mateus asked.

"She isn't going in today. We took care of that all night."

Mateus chuckled. "Good. You let me know the plan of action. I think you're right, though. Calvarro is up to something, and we need to be ready."

"Yes we do. I'm going to put some men on that. Giada will remain here, and we'll work out the job situation."

"What do you have in mind? I mean it's probably not safe there, but if she's aware of the danger and knows not to trust anyone, she could continue to work."

"I'm not feeling comfortable with that idea and with Giada returning to the job, not while that woman Julia is there and could be helping Calvarro and his cousins with whatever."

"I don't blame you. Just keep in mind how hard she has worked to achieve that job, that position."

"Understood. I'll keep you posted." Dominick eased back in the chair and rubbed his chin. What the hell was Calvarro planning?

"Dominick?"

He looked up and saw Giada standing there just wearing one of his dress shirts. She swallowed hard and looked upset. He knew she'd heard the phone call. "Morning, doll. Are you hungry?" he asked her and looked toward the kitchen where Giuseppe was making breakfast.

She slid her hands down the shirt over her thighs. "Who was that on the phone? What did you mean about me not returning to my job and about Julia?"

"Eavesdropping, Giada?" He put down the paper and sat forward in his seat.

She worried her bottom lip, and he took in the sight of her. She looked sexy, gorgeous, and so young. God, she was youthful, and after a night of sex with three men, she had a glow about her. They had done that to her by loving her. He had to do whatever was necessary to protect her.

"Come here."

She slowly walked closer to him. When she stood between his legs, he placed his hands on the sides of her knees and eased his palms up and down her legs and under the white dress shirt. She placed her hands on his shoulders when he pulled her closer and eased his palms all the way to her hips. She was naked underneath, and his cock hardened once again.

She stared at him with those gorgeous blue eyes, and her long onyx hair slid forward, and he inhaled her shampoo.

"We have things to discuss." He eased his fingers along the crack of her ass and then toward the front to her cunt. He tapped the inside of her thigh, and she stepped her feet apart, knowing what he wanted without asking. She gripped his shoulders. He stroked her pussy lips while holding her gaze.

"Do you trust me, Giada?" he asked her.

"Yes."

His heart leaped with pride and joy. She was wet, ready for him to take her again, for Andreas and Giuseppe to have her, too. She loved when they took her together. They had been so worried about her size in comparison to them and about the possibility of hurting her, but then she'd begged for more and for them to take her harder, deeper.

"Then you have to accept my orders, my ways of keeping you safe. Andreas, Giuseppe, and I won't risk you getting hurt by any man, by anyone ever. Last night, with you having to defend yourself, never should have happened." He stroked a finger up into her channel.

She gripped his shoulders. "Dominick, please. Oh."

She moaned, and he wrapped his arm around her waist and lifted her. He stroked her cunt as he continued to thrust his finger into her channel. His muscles ached from the movements and position, but he needed her again. He would never get enough of her.

He placed her onto the lower part of the counter and continued to pump his fingers into her cunt. Then he pulled them out and lowered his mouth to her pussy.

"Sweet. Giada before breakfast. Great idea, Dom," Giuseppe said and stood there watching.

Dominick shoved his pants down and aligned his cock with her pussy. "I need you."

"I need you, too. Always," she said.

He slid into her cunt as she gripped onto his forearms. Dominick gripped her hips and stroked faster. "Unbutton your top. I want to see those sexy breasts and belly ring."

She undid the buttons and let the material part.

"Gorgeous." Giuseppe reached over and tugged on her nipple.

"Giuseppe!" she cried out.

"What is going on in here?" Andreas asked, joining them, all dressed and ready for the day with his hair still wet from his shower.

Dominick stared at her face and into those gorgeous blue eyes. "You'll do what I ask, Giada. Whatever I ask you'll do, yes?"

Her lips parted, and she cried out as she came.

"Tell me. Answer me," he demanded, trying not to come yet.

"Yes, Dominick. Whatever you ask, I'll do. Yes."

"Mine. Mine." He grunted and thrust several more times and then came. He felt light-headed, overwhelmed with emotions, and he pulled her up as he slid from her cunt and squeezed her to him.

"Whatever I ask, you do. It's the only way we can protect you, the only way." He kissed her neck.

She clung to him tight. "I promise, Dominick. I will."

He looked at Andreas, who nodded with a very serious facial expression. She was everything to the three of them, everything, and she needed protection.

Chapter 12

"Where is she?" Giuseppe asked Train as he got out of the elevator at Club X and met him by the hallway.

"She's with Royce."

"I can't believe her fucking boss would fire her. She was the one who was assaulted, sexually harassed," he exclaimed.

Train agreed. "We're working on it now. Brew went to the bar where it all happened to see what he can do. She's very upset."

Giuseppe saw Giada immediately. She was by the bar with Royce and the guys. They were gathered around her, protecting her.

"Giada."

She turned and looked up with anger, not tears in her eyes. "Do you believe this crap?"

He looked at the others then at her. "No, I don't believe it." He placed his hand on her hip. She immediately hugged him and kissed his chin where she could reach. He looked at Royce and the others, squinting.

She pulled back. "I am so angry right now. I didn't even want to come here first. I wanted to go by Carlitto's. I know a bartender there. He was working the other night when this happened. I know they have surveillance videos and stuff. They probably have it on tape unless Calvarro and his cousins, the slimy snakes, destroyed those tapes. God, I wish I was taller. I could have hit his nose and broken it. Grrr." She carried on, and he chuckled.

"I can't get over this reaction, Giada."

"What? Why? You expect me to do what, cry? Are you kidding me? Do you realize how hard I worked to get that job and position?

How many hours and weekends and shitty meetings with perverted assholes?" She shook her head.

He pulled her back in front of him and cupped her cheeks. Narrowing his eyes at her, he held her gaze. "Perverted assholes?"

"Duh! Of course perverted assholes, and other men who thought they could seal the deals better than me. I made a lot of money for that company, and they aren't getting away with this. No way," she stated firmly.

"Calm down and let us handle this. Brew is already doing his thing."

"What thing?" she asked.

"Don't worry about it, Giada. You were in the right. You'll get that job back and an apology," Train told her.

"Knowing Brew, she'll get more than that," Royce said and winked at her.

Giuseppe held her around her waist from behind, and she leaned back against him.

"Why not have a drink? What are you in the mood for?" Royce asked her.

"A martini. Make it a double."

Giuseppe whispered into her ear. "We have to stay late. We have things going on here tonight."

"Well, I can stay late with you. I don't have a job right now," she said.

He gave her a kiss on her temple. "It will work out. You'll see," he told her, but he wondered if it would and couldn't help but feel hopeful it didn't. She could be around them a lot more and move in with them quickly. He didn't want her out of his sight, and working or going out with her friends did just that.

* * * *

"So, how is the whole leave-of-absence thing going?" Fina asked Giada as they walked around the boutique.

They were both looking for dresses to wear to Club Magique next week. Caprice was performing, and then they were all going to enjoy a little dancing and hanging out with their men.

"It's actually pretty fun. I slept in late two days, and by Wednesday, I was going insane I was so bored. I never realized how much responsibility I had with my job and how all-consuming it was."

"So go back. You got the perfect package and deal after Brew got through with your bosses," Fina said to her.

Giada smiled. "Brew was awesome, and with the bonus I got, never mind the flexible schedule, of course I'm going back. Next week actually. I just haven't told the guys yet."

"Why not?" Fina asked as she pulled a blue dress off the rack and looked at it.

"Well," Giada said and looked around them to make sure no one could hear them talking. The boutique was a little crowded. So much so that Train and Brew waited outside. "They kind of like keeping me...accessible." She smiled.

"Oh, isn't that just so sexy. You doing them in their offices."

Giada gave Fina's arm a slap.

"You should just move in with them. You're practically living in their penthouse as is." Fina put back the blue dress.

"I know. I was just hung up on the whole time-factor thing and thinking it was too soon, worried it could get screwed up."

"Well, if they've dealt with you the last week bored out of your mind, they'll probably survive you living with them."

"Nice, Fina," she said, and Fina laughed. "Lunch?"

"Sure. I can't seem to find anything here."

"Me either. Maybe we can hit Merlot's after lunch."

"Will Brew and Train mind?"

"I don't think so. Something is going on at the club. They've been texting back and forth, and Brew keeps taking pictures of me. That means the guys are worried."

"Oh no. Is it something serious?"

"I don't think so, Fina, but I know they weren't happy to find out that not only was Julia working for Calvarro but so was Monterro, who, by the way, lost his job once Brew got through with Davis. He had no idea what was going on or what I was put through. I kind of feel funny going back to work and dealing with the gossip, yet my new position, which I earned, should leave me with less time in the office and more time out and about or working from home."

"The guys will like that."

"They will, and I can't wait to tell them when I let them know I'm going back to work next week."

"Being sneaky, huh? Using the work-from-home thing to get them to accept your early decision?"

"You know me so well."

"Yes, I do," Fina said, and they laughed.

Thirty minutes later they were eating lunch and enjoying the day when Fina grabbed her arm.

"Oh no." She pointed.

Giada looked behind her and saw Uncle Les by the side entryway. He waved at her to come over. She shook her head and turned back around.

"Are you not talking to him still?" Fina asked.

"He wants me to break things off with Andreas, Giuseppe, and Dominick. He's been against them from the start and keeps telling me that they mean me harm. It's been a few weeks since I last saw or heard from him."

"Well, he's coming over."

Giada saw Train and Brew coming, too. "Oh no." She stood and turned around. "Uncle Les, what are you doing here? I don't want any trouble."

He stared at her. "We need to talk."

"There's nothing to talk to her about. If you're here to cause trouble, please leave," Brew said to him.

"I'm not leaving. She's my niece. I'm her family. What are you to her?" he scolded them.

Brew raised one eyebrow at Uncle Les and exhaled, unsure how to handle the older man. He looked at Giada.

"It's okay, Brew. Let him stay and we'll talk, but if he causes trouble, he's done."

"Are you sure, Giada? You don't need any extra aggravation," Train said to her as Brew pulled out his cell phone. He was more than likely calling Dominick.

"Yes," she said.

Uncle Les stared at the two guards walked away.

"What do you want to talk about?" Giada asked him.

He looked at her and exhaled, taking the seat beside her. He looked exhausted. He took her hand and held it. "I worry about you. I don't like this, them, and how there's more than one of them wanting you intimately."

She gulped. It wasn't easy to explain the power of a ménage, the commitment involved. "Uncle Les, Andreas, Dominick, and Giuseppe are good men, and they care about me. They love me."

He shook his head. "They aren't loyal to you. Women throw themselves at them all the time. I heard they got you fired from your job, too, that Andreas cheated on you."

She shook her head and pulled her hand from his. "No, Uncle Les. That was a misunderstanding, a setup actually, and Andreas didn't cheat on me."

He lowered his head and inched closer. "I don't like this. I had a plan of getting this job, making really good money and talking care of you, paying you back for all you've done to help me."

She saw the emotion in his eyes and felt him shaking. Her eyes filled up with tears. "Uncle Les, you don't need to take care of me or pay me back. Take care of yourself. Get that job, make your money, and get a better life. Maybe quit drinking and messing around in bad stuff that will only get you into trouble, beaten up, or worse. I don't want to get another call from some bartender that you were roughed up and left for dead. I don't."

"If I get this job, we'll both be rich. We'll both have more money than we'll know what to do with. You don't need to settle for this kind of relationship."

"Uncle Les, the money doesn't matter. I have plenty of money. I've worked very hard. I love them, and I'm going to be moving in with them next week."

He pulled back and stared at her. "What would Jimmy say?"

Tears filled her eyes. "He would be happy for her, knowing she had three great men who would protect her, provide for her, and love her fully," Fina chimed in.

Thank God because if Giada had to speak, she was going to cry. She had a bad feeling, an empty feeling in her gut telling her that the uncle she once had would be gone after today. He wouldn't mean anything to her anymore. His focus had always been money—making money, getting rich, becoming something he wasn't willing to work hard for but instead get someway somehow and with no care of the consequences.

"Money isn't everything, Uncle Les."

He narrowed his eyes at her. "It is to me. Money gets you things you never had before. Can give you power, control, and even make dreams a reality. All I've ever done was try to make more money and to care for you so you weren't alone, especially after Jimmy died. Instead, you made it on your own, and now you're going to throw it all away?" He raised his voice.

She shook her head. She felt sick to her stomach, but something inside of her wouldn't just push him away and tell him she hated him and to never come near her again. He was her only family. She reached over and took his hand.

"They can't protect you like Jimmy did," he said to her.

"Uncle Les, I love them, and they love me."

"They say they love you because they want to own every part of you. That's what these men do. I can't stand to think of the pain, the heartache you'll feel when they push you aside, treat you like some material thing instead of the beautiful, smart woman you are."

He gulped, and she nearly cried. "Uncle Les, I want you in my life. I do. You're my only family, but if you can't accept my men, then I can't let you remain part of my life. I can't."

He stared at her and exhaled. He didn't say a word for a few moments, and it was unnerving. He glanced toward Brew and Train, who remained close by watching ready to do whatever was needed to protect her.

Then he looked at her. "We're all the family we got, Giada. I guess you give me no choice."

She squinted ta him, not certain what that meant.

"I don't want you to hate me because I disagree with this relationship. It will take time to get used to this. I'll fear them hurting you, and I can't help that, you know?" He gave her a small smile.

She nodded. "It's a beginning, Uncle Les. You'll see how much they care and love me. You'll see."

He nodded, and then she called over the waiter to bring Uncle Les something to drink and made him order some lunch. He looked tired and weak. She glanced at Fina, who gave her a reassuring smile, and then asked Uncle Les about Queens and whether that small little bakery was still up and running and making those jelly-filled pastries she adored.

Giada couldn't help but smile. This could work out. She could have her only family—her uncle—in her life, three great men who loved her and adored her, and surround herself with her friends and those people who cared about her and supported her in this ménage relationship. Suddenly she was feeling pretty optimistic.

* * * *

Dominick walked into the bathroom in the penthouse and saw Giada in the shower. He'd worried about her all day and how her uncle had come to see her and cause some shit. He understood that her uncle would accept them as her lovers, her men, because he didn't want to lose his only relative. Giada needed that, too, to hold on to the past, a family connection, and especially after losing Jimmy.

He swallowed hard. He didn't like feeling a little jealous of a dead man. He understood the connection, the bond she had with the man she'd loved and thought she would marry and have children with. It just seemed to bother him more, not less. He glanced at his watch. They would be late to the dinner party. There would be no way to avoid it, not as he undressed and took in the sight of her curves, the way her long onyx locks clung to her hips, right above her ass.

His dick hardened as he slowly joined her, prepared to reprimand her for not hearing him enter or see him watching her luscious body. As he slid in behind her and ran his palms up her hips and under her arms to her breasts, she hadn't jerked or acted surprised.

"I was wondering when you would join me, Dominick."

He kissed her neck. "You knew I was there?"

She moaned softly as he sucked a little harder on her neck. "I always know when one of you are near. I feel it. Everywhere," she whispered.

He slid his palm along her belly, over the belly ring and taut muscles then down to her pussy. "Everywhere?" he asked, easing his digit into her cunt.

She parted her thighs and bent so obediently and with need. "Everywhere."

He eased back, sliding his other hand along her neck and spine, pressing her down. "I need in—now." He removed his fingers, bent slightly, and eased his hard, thick shaft into her cunt from behind. Her palms were pressed against the wall, her shoulder and back muscles so sexy and feminine. He couldn't help but ease out and then slowly push into her as he massaged her body everywhere he could reach.

"Fuck, I missed you today. I can't stand being apart from you."

"I know, Dominick. I feel that way, too."

He stroked a little faster. "I can't go on like this, Giada. I need to know where you are at all times and that you're living here in the penthouse and not in your apartment. I can't take it, baby." He thrust faster, gripped her hips, and stroked into her with vigor and need.

"Oh, Dominick. Oh God, this is amazing. I love you so much. I can't live without with you, Andreas, and Giuseppe."

"Hot damn, we feel the same way," Giuseppe chimed in.

He and Andreas were there undressing. Dominick looked at them as he thrust into her pussy. They looked just as needy as he felt.

"She's ours," he said and then slid his hands along her back to her shoulders, using them as leverage to thrust into her deeply. She moaned and tightened up. He felt her pussy muscles grip his cock, and he could hardly keep up the deep, hard strokes when she came and he followed.

"Oh, Giada. Damn." He slid from her pussy, turned her around, lifted her into his arms, and kissed her. He felt dizzy as he pressed her back against the wall and then moved his lips to her neck and just breathed in her scent and felt her wet skin as the water cascaded over it.

* * * *

Andreas sat on the seat in the shower and pulled her into his arms. He couldn't believe how much he'd missed her today and worried about her, especially after her uncle showed up and made her emotional. Brew and Train had kept them abreast of the situation, but it only made them more desperate to have her in their sights and in their arms where she was safest. He stroked her cheek as she straddled his waist and kissed him. She moaned a second later as Giuseppe moved in behind her and began to press lube to her ass. Dominick looked on after passing Giuseppe the tube.

"Take me inside of you, woman. We need you together."

Her lips parted as she held on to his shoulders. He stared at her and felt her grip his cock and slide her hot, wet cunt down it. He closed his eyes a moment, feeling how good it felt to have her, to be buried deep inside of her. It was exceptional and made life seem perfect and like nothing else mattered. He slid his hands up to her breasts and cupped them. She gripped his shoulders and began to lift up and down on his shaft then gasped.

"So fucking tight. I thought about this ass a lot today and fucking it." Giuseppe slowly pushed into her ass from behind.

It was a little tight in the shower, but because of her petite size and their large sizes, one of them sitting on the bench and one standing seemed to work out perfectly. Another indicator of how perfect this relationship and combination was.

"Oh God, Giada, you kill me. I can't even move. I feel like coming already, watching my cock disappearing into this sexy, tight ass. Fuck." Giuseppe smacked her ass.

"Giuseppe." She looked over her shoulder, only for Giuseppe to kiss her hard on the mouth and grip her hair.

It sent Andreas over the edge, too, and he gripped her hips and thrust upward as Giuseppe thrust into her ass in sync to his thrusts. The water fell over them, landing on her perfect skin, her lush breasts, and as her lips parted, her eyes widened, showing him those gorgeous blue eyes he adored, and she came, gasping for breath.

"Fuck," Giuseppe shouted and thrust fast, really fast, into her ass, and then he came.

He pulled out and gripped the stone-tiled walls as Andreas stood, cupped her ass, turned her against the wall, and thrust into her fully. He kissed her mouth, ravaged it as he continued to sink his cock deeper and faster into his woman's pussy. He was feeling so out of control, and when their lips parted, Giada screamed out, gripped his hair, and grunted, coming again. He thrust and stroked and then roared, shoving hard against her as he came. He apologized for being so rough as he kissed her neck, her chin, and her lips.

"No apologies, Andreas. I loved it. I love how possessive each of you is and how you make my body somehow want more and more. I love it," she said, out of breath.

He squeezed her tight and held her there a little longer.

"We are going to be so fucking late it isn't even funny," Dominick stated, walking into the bathroom buttoning his shirt cuffs and adding cuff links.

Andreas set her down and turned off the water. He kept a hand on her hip as Giuseppe opened up a big towel and then pulled her into his arms and hugged her tight.

"Do we have to go, Dominick? Can't we just stay here and…snuggle?" she asked.

Andreas chuckled as Dominick looked at her with a firm expression.

"Snuggle?" he asked, straight-faced.

She used the towel to dry her hair, showing off her sexy curves and bare breasts as she did it. "Oh, don't go saying it like it's so terrible and you hate it. I know the truth, Dominick Coglonie, and you love to snuggle with me."

She gave Dominick a sassy look as she walked by him. Dominick gave her ass a hard smack.

"Hey." She reached back to caress where he'd spanked her.

"I love giving you a good spanking more, so move it, woman," he scolded.

She hurried out of the room. Andreas laughed, and so did Giuseppe. Dominick exhaled.

"We can't fight it either, Dominick. She's incredible," Andreas said.

They all agreed and got ready for the dinner party at Club Merchant.

Chapter 13

"We need to talk. Now," Fedarro said to Dominick, Andreas, and Giuseppe.

Dominick looked toward Train and Brew, who were standing nearby. He caught their attention, pointed at his eyes, and then at Giada, indicating for them to watch over her, and both men nodded. They all headed out of the main area where it was less crowded and to one of the rooms.

"What's going on?" Andreas asked as Fedarro and Mateus joined them.

"Vinny called. He was checking on a potential problem with one of the guys we count on to watch the truck shipments when a trailer pulled in he didn't recognize. Anyway, Vinny had Morano's guy Corrano with him, and then they were going to head here afterward, but when he started asking about the shipment, the guy there got all nervous and tried blowing it off," Fedarro stated.

"So what was in it? He found out right?" Dominick asked.

"Women."

"What?" Giuseppe asked.

"A fucking trailer of women. Some looked half dead from malnourishment, others battered and, Vinny said, definitely raped. Like sex slaves of some shit. Trafficking women is bad, evil, dirty business that we've avoided and helped destroy in our area. This is serious."

"What the fuck?" Dominick raised his voice with his hands on his hips and began to pace.

"I know. This is fucking bad. We couldn't exactly call the cops because of the other things we have there, but either someone is planting them for us to get busted or we didn't really have full control of that operation there. Vinny thinks the latter," Mateus stated.

"Why? That's been a warehouse of ours for years," Giuseppe added.

"Exactly, and when Vinny started questioning the guy, he rambled on about getting paid on the side, and some big shot from out of the country, Cuba or some shit, paid him and a few other men to do these shipments," Mateus told them.

"This could have landed all of us in fucking jail," Dominick said to them, and they all agreed.

"Where are the women now? Vinny got them help? Someplace safe?" Andreas asked.

"Adelina had a hookup in the NYPD. They're all at the hospital after the truck was reported sitting in an abandoned parking lot, a few blocks away from the ER," Mateus said, and Dominick exhaled.

"Are you thinking it was Calvarro? We know he's dabbled in sex trafficking for years. Could be he was trying to continue that business since we took the importing stuff out from under him or wanted to get us busted? I'm thinking either one is fucking unacceptable. He's a problem," Dominick stated.

"He's a serious problem, so much so that I've heard from Dmitri, who heard from Nicolai, that there's buzz of some fucking asshole making deals, finagling shit to take us out," Fedarro told him.

"Take us out? Who the fuck would that be?" Dominick asked.

"Don't know, but we need to figure this shit out fast and decide what to do about Calvarro. At this point any of our enemies could strike and blindside us. We don't know who set out to destroy this operation and joint deal, but we'd better figure it out fast, or it could be disastrous," Fedarro said to him.

"Agreed. Maybe we need to up the security guys and pull in more seasoned military men from Blood Line Securities instead of the regulars. Every shipment in and out needs to be verified and checked before it even enters the gates of all the warehouses," Andreas said to them.

"Agreed. It's going to take extra time but will be well worth it. I'd say watch yourselves and keep your eyes and ears open. Someone wants this deal, our business destroyed. That isn't going to happen," Fedarro said firmly.

Dominick swallowed hard. His gut clenched. Who was initiating this attack on them, and why?

* * * *

Giada glanced down at her cell phone and saw that it was Uncle Les calling. She walked from the room to the hallway and answered. "Hello?"

"Giada, I need a favor."

She felt the hand on her shoulder. It was Brew. "I'm okay, Brew. Just taking the call in here where it's quieter."

"Who is it?" he asked.

"Uncle Les." She rolled her eyes. "Let me take this back here, okay?"

"Whatever." Brew walked down the hall to the entryway and stood guard. She stepped to the side right out of sight of him.

"What's going on? I'm at a party right now."

"I know. Club Merchant. I'm in a jam. Any way I can get a hundred dollars from you?"

"A hundred? For what?"

"I kind of made a bet, and well, I need a hundred to cover things."

"I'm at a party, Uncle Les."

"I know. You don't have to leave the party. Just meet me."

"Where?" she asked, looking around her.

"The exit door by the ladies' room."

She looked back to where Brew was. He was going to be pissed and so were her men if they knew that Uncle Les had asked her for money. He never seemed to have any and always asked her for help. The man was obsessed with making it big and doing it fast. His life was a mess. He'd never really accomplished anything because his focus was always money, money, money, the next big deal, a way to hit it big.

"This is the last time, Uncle Les."

"Okay. I promise. Just come to the exit door—alone."

He didn't have to worry about that. She wouldn't have Brew come with her and then tell her men she'd given her uncle a hundred dollars and then hear them reprimand her and get upset. They already didn't like her uncle.

She hurried down the hallway and to the exit door. She pulled the money from her purse and then opened the door. The second it opened, Uncle Les pulled her out and took her hand.

"What are you doing?" she demanded.

"Saving you. Making things right. We're going to be rich, Giada, rich, and you'll be well taken care of. He can't wait to make you his. He doesn't even care about your indiscretions."

"Have you been drinking? What in God's name are you—"

She felt the prick to her neck, turned, and saw some big, very tan man standing there. He caught her and lifted her up into his arms as her body went numb.

"Move," he said.

An SUV pulled up slowly, quietly and they took her into the back seat, Uncle Les, too.

"Stop!" she heard Brew yell, and then gunfire went off around her. She screamed out for help but couldn't move.

"No. No please don't do this. Brew, help me!" she screamed and saw the back door to Merchant shove open, and men, Train and others, run out firing their weapons. One of the men taking her got hit as the doors closed and the SUV sped off.

She felt the tears roll down her cheeks as she stared at Uncle Les, who now looked a little scared. He tapped her hand.

"It's the right thing to do. To save you, Giada. You'll see."

* * * *

"I want everyone on this. Everyone!" Dominick yelled as they all gathered around the back room at Club Merchant.

"Her own fucking uncle was in on whatever the fuck is happening. That asshole. I didn't like him from the start," Brew said as he sat in the chair and Collin Fiorre took care of the flesh wound Brew had gotten as the men who'd taken Giada fired upon him.

"We're checking out all the places we can for the guy that Train shot. He'll need serious medical attention," Royce told them.

"I want that guy from the warehouse brought in for questioning. This has something to do with Giada being taken, as well. Someone, Calvarro or someone else, is behind this," Dominick said to them.

"Agreed. We can try to push and put the word out, too, on this. Everything we can, Dominick," Fedarro said to him.

"What do we have to go by from the guy at the warehouse?" Andreas asked.

"He said the guy who offered him and others money was Cuban or something. Not from around here," Mateus said to them.

Andreas looked at Royce. "We have to do everything we can to find her, and since we don't know who is behind this, we need to backtrack and investigate all angles, aspects, everything. I'm thinking all this shit started happening around the takeover of the cigar industry, importing and exporting. Plus, we got involved with Giada, and Calvarro's cousins just happened to be starting investment in her bank. I want a full investigation on them, too. I want every single client she has been in contact with, every appointment with every potential client in the last year."

"I can assist with that. Her boss, Davis, would know. Maybe Royce can find Monterro Spain. He was fired after what happened with Giada. He could have gotten paid to ensure it was Giada who worked with Alajandro and Toro, if this is all connected to Calvarro," Brew added.

'We'll get on it now, Andreas," Royce said, and he and Train exited the room.

Dominick looked at Andreas and Giuseppe as the others made plans and started doing their thing to find Giada and quickly.

"We'll find her, and when we do, whoever is responsible will go down," Fedarro promised him, and Dominick nodded.

His worry was for Giada. She was petite, feminine, and from the surveillance tapes, it looked as if they'd drugged her.

"Whoever did this might have known her capabilities with martial arts and self-defense. They drugged her immediately," Dominick stated.

"Definitely why they did it, which leads back to Alajandro, Toro, and Calvarro," Andreas said.

"Grab them and bring them in for questioning, too," Giuseppe stated firmly.

Then Dominick's cell phone rang. He looked at it and then up at everyone as he answered. "Dmitri?"

"Tell me what you need. Where you are with this?"

"Nowhere. We're banging our heads together wondering where this is coming from." He explained where they were and about dealing with Calvarro and his cousins.

"I can find out exactly where those women were taken from and who was behind that shipment," Dmitri told him.

"You can?" he asked, shocked.

"I will look into that. I'm sending Andriy, Paulo, and Hadeon there. They should arrive in a few hours. They will be of great use to you."

"Thank you, Dmitri. We appreciate your help in this."

"Rayanna is concerned for Giada. Anything you need we will help with."

"Thank you, and we'll keep you posted," Dominick stated and ended the call. "Dmitri is sending Hadeon, Paulo and Andriy."

"Good. We'll need them. They have resources we don't. Anyone can have her and take her anywhere," Giuseppe said.

"Uncle Les's house. Let me grab some guys and head there to look around and see if he left any indication of his plan. Maybe we'll get lucky." Andreas headed out of the room.

"Who wants to go along for a ride to Cha Cha Cabana with Giuseppe and me? We want answers, and we want them now," Dominick said.

Fedarro and Mateus nodded. "We'll get things ready," Fedarro said, and they prepared to confront Calvarro and find out what he knew about Giada's abduction.

He was prepared to do what was necessary to get the fucker to talk.

* * * *

Giada was conscious, but she couldn't move a muscle. She was petrified at the situation, not knowing what was happening, who these men were, and how her uncle could be part of this. She listened as Uncle Les spoke to the men.

"What are we doing next? Where's the money? Are you taking her to Cuba?" he rambled on.

"Just shut up," one of the men yelled at him. He was facing forward, holding a large gun, some semiautomatic type of rifle in his arms, and it leaned against his shoulder.

"I was told I would get money for bringing her to you. He said he would take care of her and make it so the Coglonie men would never get their hands on her again."

"You'll get your money. That's what you wanted from the start—money," he snapped at Uncle Les.

She couldn't believe what she was hearing. Her uncle had sold her out, helped to abduct her. Who was in charge of this? What was it about? She thought of Calvarro, Alajandro, and Toro. Were they a part of this?

She thought about her men and about Brew and Train. She shouldn't have walked to the door without Brew. Her men were going to be angry with her. How stupid was she? She had to realize that they were made men, men with enemies who wanted to hurt them, hell, hurt people important to them. That was why her men demanded the control they did over her. Was it too late? Would she ever see them again? She cried more.

"This wasn't the deal," Uncle Les said.

The SUV stopped short. She nearly rolled off the seat, but the guy with the gun held her thigh in place. She couldn't even feel that either. She just saw his hand go there. It was the craziest sensation.

The door opened, and another man, one with a beard and pissed-off look, pulled Uncle Les from the vehicle. She looked and heard the exchange of words.

"He promised me money!" Uncle Les yelled.

"You'll get it once you complete the other part of the plan."

"What other part of the plan?" Uncle Les demanded to know.

"The part where you die knowing that you sold your niece out for money to her men's enemies and now her freedom is over."

She heard the shot from the gun, and Uncle Les fell backward. The guy got back into the SUV.

"Asshole," he said, and they sped off.

They shot her uncle. They promised him money, and he sold her out to them?

"Don't cry, Giada," the one guy said to her, but she couldn't move to see him. "Money is the route to all evil. He got what was coming to him."

She closed her eyes and prayed that her men would find her. She couldn't believe this. Who were these men? Where were they taking her? How could her uncle have done this? She cried until exhaustion or the high of whatever they'd given her had kicked in.

* * * *

"Do you believe this? Look at all this stuff. Her uncle has been monitoring her every move. Keeping track of her schedule, the route she takes to work. Everything," Logic said to Andreas.

They were looking through the place but had come up with nothing but his surveillance of Giada. Andreas felt sick. "I didn't like that guy from the moment he came into the hospital and demanded we leave her."

"He has a short fuse, Andreas. We saw his reaction at Giada's apartment that night when you guys were providing protection. He nearly lost it then. Whoever took her knew that he would be easily manipulated."

"Yet she wanted to forgive him, keep him in her life as the only family she has, and he backstabs her? Sells her out? For what?" Andreas asked.

"Money, probably," Sunny said as he dumped over a garbage bag filled with overdue bills.

"Damn. That would make a person do something evil and stupid," Logic said as he looked at the bills.

"His own niece, though?" Sunny added and shook his head.

Andreas's cell phone rang. "Adelina, what's going on? Got anything for me?" Andreas asked and looked at Sunny. "When and where? … So they'll let us know? … Great, thank you." He disconnected the call. "Uncle Les was found a few blocks from the airport. He's been shot and isn't coherent. Fedarro is bringing him to a special location to question him. She said that he isn't going to make it, but they're hoping to keep him alive long enough to get names."

"Good. The son of a bitch should die a miserable death for what he did," Sunny said.

"We should head out of here. Anything from Brew yet, Logic?" Andreas asked.

"No."

"Where the hell is that guy they questioned about the delivery the other night? How come they can't find him?" Andreas asked, hoping he could get his hands on that guy and get something concrete that could help.

"Either he's in hiding or whoever is operating this situation took him out," Logic said.

Andreas hoped not. They had no leads, and time just kept ticking away.

* * * *

"I need her cleaned up and ready for my cousin to arrive. You're over a day late."

"We had some trouble at the airport and needed to divert the plane as a precaution. Apparently her uncle's body was found by some men working for the Costanza family."

"I thought we said to kill her uncle."

"You said make him suffer for selling out Giada. We did. Shot him in a spot that would cause major internal bleeding. I'm surprised he was alive when they found him."

"If he talks, then we have less time to enjoy fucking with the Coglonies. Get the staff to clean her up and put her in something my cousin will love her in."

"Yes, sir."

* * * *

Giada felt the very warm air against her skin. She blinked her eyes open and squinted at the sunlight coming through from the sliding doors that were wide open. She heard sounds that reminded her of a tropical place, and she went to move, felt how difficult it was, and moaned. She looked down at her hands, arms, and body. She was dressed in a strapless romper in blue. There was beading along the top and the skirt short with beading along the bottom. She felt sick to her stomach. Someone had undressed her and put her in this. Had they touched her? Raped her? She tried to focus on how her body felt.

She tried moving and, in doing so, fell from the bed onto the floor. She cried out. The noise was loud as she hit the wooden flooring. She heard heavy footsteps and was trying to push herself up off the floor when the door opened.

"Shit. You need to be on the bed and looking perfect, not bruised up. He won't be happy," the guy said in annoyance. He lifted her into his arms and placed her back onto the bed. He fixed the skirt of the romper.

"Help me. Where am I?" She blinked her heavy eyelids.

The man licked his lips. "Damn if you weren't taken, boy, would I be working on getting you used to my touch."

He stroked her cheek. She turned away. He looked to be in his thirties, Hispanic with an accent.

"Miami, he's here."

She heard another man's voice, and then this guy they called Miami smiled.

"Your man is here." He winked and stood from the bed.

"Stay just like that. You look perfect." He went to the door. She heard him greet the other man hello.

"In there. She's still weak from the drugs."

"Good."

She thought she recognized the voice. Then she heard him approach the doorway, and she looked, waiting to see who had taken her from her men and accomplished all of this. She gaped, and her heart felt as though it dropped to her belly.

"Emanuel Cortez. Crown Royal."

* * * *

Emanuel Cortez didn't smile, despite the pleasure he felt at seeing Giada here in Cuba and lying on the bed. He placed his hands on his hips as she stared at him in shock and confusion. He'd had a long trip. Everything was in place. Shortly the Coglonie family would know that it was he who had taken their precious, beautiful woman from them, see how they liked losing something, someone important to them, just like how they'd taken his brother from him.

"I don't understand," she whispered.

He stood by the bed looking down at her petite figure, her sexy thighs, her full breasts, and her long, gorgeous locks of hair. Those stunning blue eyes and angelic face filled with fear made him feel the taste of success, of vengeance on his lips. He reached out and stroked her bare shoulder. She tried pulling back, but the drugs still made her weak. She needed to remain weak, compliant to his orders and instruction.

"Don't resist, Giada. I don't want to hurt you or ruin this perfect body in any way." He stroked along her hip and down her thigh. He grazed over her groin and her mound, and she tried turning away.

"Don't touch me."

"Oh, I will be touching you, and your men will see it." He pointed to the camera in the corner of the room. She looked shocked as though she hadn't noticed it was there. "We'll be keeping a close watch on you, me especially, since this is my bedroom and now yours, too."

"No. Please don't rape me. Please," she said to him as tears rolled down her cheeks.

"Tsk, tsk." He stroked the tears away. "I have never raped a woman before, and I'm not about to start now. Eventually, though, you'll be mine and will accept me freely, or there will be hell to pay."

She shook her head.

"Oh, don't worry about it now, Giada. We've got time on our side. And to think we nearly lost the opportunity to grab you. Good old Uncle Les." He smiled.

She shook her head.

"Oh wait, that's right. He's dead." He leaned one arm over her waist and came closer to her lips. She tightened up but didn't move her arms to stop him. Apparently the drugs worked for quite some time on her. She was small.

He stroked her jaw and kept his hand and arm by her breast. "You are so gorgeous. No wonder all three of them wanted you. You're a goddess, Giada, and now you're mine.'

"Never," she whispered.

He gripped her jaw, and she gasped. "You'll see. Now, you'll need to eat, perhaps use the bathroom, and then join me on our first night in paradise. Oh, and don't think about trying to escape. I have numerous guards surrounding the perimeter of the island, all around the perimeter of the house, and a surveillance system that allows my guards to not only see and hear everything but also alert them to intruders a good half a mile away. More than enough time for me to escape with you if anyone was so stupid as to try and get through the security that's in place."

"Why are you doing this? Why me?"

"Oh, we'll talk about that over dinner, as well as the rules. No time to waste, Giada. Tonight we make the first tape and send it to your friends, the Coglonies."

He leaned lower and went to kiss her lips, but she tried turning away. He gripped her jaw tight. "Cooperation is key, or your quarters during the day will not be pleasant at all. There's a lot of dangers outside these doors, both nature and man. You won't survive very long at all."

* * * *

"Emanuel Cortez," Brew said to all of them as they gathered inside of the penthouse.

"Fuck," Andreas stated.

Dominick remained straight-faced.

Giuseppe looked at Brew. "What did you find out?"

"He came to see her two weeks ago. They met for a short time in her office and then discussed meeting again to go over him being a potential client."

"Ballsy," Fedarro said, knowing the situation and what had happened a few years ago.

None of them even thought Emanuel was alive. He wasn't connected with Raoul.

"Who is this guy Cortez?" Hadeon, one of Dmitri's guys, asked.

"A Cuban dealer. His brother, Raoul, tried to double-cross Fedarro and his family and ours in a joint operation. Sent in some enforcers to eliminate us for a takeover. We caught wind of it, thanks to Andreas and his connections. As they came in to attack, Raoul went after me," Dominick said to them.

He didn't have to give details to these men. They realized he'd killed Raoul.

"So his brother, Emanuel, got away, waited three years to seek his revenge against you, and now he takes your woman." Andriy shook his head.

"He knows she is important to the three of them. He's been watching us or having us watched. We have to find him. The longer he has Giada, the worse he can do to her," Fedarro said.

They all looked grim. Dominick felt so angry and helpless. His Giada must be so scared. He clenched his teeth.

"We need to put the pressure on. His cousin Miami Cortez is one of the operators of the Bay Bloods. It could mean getting our fucking hands real dirty, but I'm so fucking angry right now I'm up for a bit of ass kicking to get answers," Andreas said to them.

"What exactly do you want to do, Andreas? Start a fucking mini blood war with one of the biggest drug gangs in Harlem?" Mateus asked him.

Dominick looked at Andreas as he eyed everyone in the room— all their men, their friends and family, their partners in business.

"No, just fuck them up enough to let them know that, at any time, we can come in and take the fuck over. That we mean business, and if their leader, Yovan Vega, wants to protect Miami, Emanuel, and anyone else who took our woman, then he and the Bay Bloods get to suffer, too."

Dominick was already formulating a plan. "We may not even have to start knocking down doors and bringing so much attention to the streets." Dominick looked at Fedarro. He didn't need to say a word as Fedarro looked at Sunny and Vinny.

"To protect that bit of resource, I say we still go in and kick some ass right now, tonight. Then we let that special resource do what can be done," Sunny suggested.

"Agreed. Let's do this. Let's take a group, Andreas, and hit up the Bay Blood gang. Another group hit up Cha Cha Cabana, and another one find Calvarro and interrogate the shit out of him while our other teams infiltrate Emanuel's financial resources. We aren't going to take this sitting down," Dominick stated.

They agreed, and everyone headed out. There would be no sleeping tonight, not any time soon, and not until Giada was safe and alive in his arms.

Chapter 14

A week—a whole fucking week—and no exact location on Emanuel, just that he was in Cuba. Hadeon, Paulo, and Andriy were getting closer and in contact with a team associated with Nicolai. The Mulichecks were married to Nicolai's daughter, Malayna. They were soldiers, hunters, and men who could infiltrate even the most high-tech security facilities out there. They knew their shit and had ways of finding out where people were. They were getting closer.

"I can't take this much longer," Giuseppe said as he ran his fingers through his hair.

Giuseppe, Dominick, Andreas, Brew, Royce, Train, and Dmitri's men were sitting in the office when Dominick got an alert on his phone. A private number. *Check your e-mail.*

He stood and walked over to the desk and got onto the computer and his e-mail. He had three screens on his desk, and he saw a link to a video. He hit the button, and he felt his heart drop to his stomach.

The sound of Emanuel's voice echoed in the office, and Giuseppe and Andreas approached along with the others.

He couldn't believe it. Emanuel was lying on a bed with Giada. He was touching her, stroking her, and she was lying there, tears streaming from her cheeks as Emanuel taunted them through the camera.

"She is so beautiful. Obedient, too, when she's drugged like this," Emanuel said to the camera. Emanuel cupped her breast as he inhaled against Giada's neck. "She smells incredible, like heaven. No wonder you, your brother, and your cousin care so much about her. She's addicting."

He then leaned up and licked her lips, down her neck, and over her breast. They watched in horror.

"I want you to know, Dominick, that since we've been here, she sleeps right by my side where I can protect her and hold her close. I bet you're going to miss that, having her nice, round ass pressed up against you. Now it's up against me. She's mine now, Dominick. Mine to control, to train, to spend as much time with as I want. It's sweet revenge, Dominick, on you and those asshole friends of yours. You're never going to see her again. Never going to touch what is mine. How does that feel?"

The screen went black, and Dominick just stared at it. The sound of a roar and a chair being thrown had Dominick looking up to see Andreas in a rage. Hadeon grabbed onto him.

"We'll find them. I promise, Andreas. We will find them."

"When? When, Hadeon? After he rapes her several times? Traumatizes her? Drugs her up? You saw her. She's helpless and scared, and we did this to her," Andreas said and walked out of the room.

Dominick tried breathing through the anger. Giuseppe turned away and faced the window. Their friends, their guards, and their family had seen and heard the video, too.

"Send a copy of that to Star," Hadeon stated.

"What? No, I don't want a bunch of people seeing that video."

"Dominick, they have their resources, their ways of finding shit, seeing things other people wouldn't. They may be able to find something on that video."

Dominick clenched his teeth and felt as though he could hardly catch a breath. He forwarded the video to the e-mail address Hadeon told him to as Hadeon spoke on the phone with Star. Poor Giada. When he got his hands on Emanuel, he would be sure to kill him.

* * * *

Giuseppe stared at the screen and then forwarded the video to Star. Three more days and nights of videos and still no concrete location. This video worse than the others. Now Emanuel lay in bed with Giada naked. She looked ill, withdrawn, white, and thinner. She was dying there. He was torturing her and making them watch it. This time he even scanned the beach, the room they were in, and showed the classy-style place they stayed as he threatened to take from her body in every room in the place. He felt sick.

The door to the office shoved open. "Did you see it?" Andreas asked him in an uproar.

Giuseppe nodded.

"I can't stand here and do nothing. I want and need to hunt. I want to go to fucking Cuba and track the motherfucker down and kill him and his crew of shit," Andreas yelled.

"Why are your knuckles all bloody?" Giuseppe asked.

"I had a little conversation with Yovan Vega. He swears to not know a thing about this operation or whether Miami is involved. He said Miami left the gang six months ago," Andreas told him.

"That's true, and right now Hadeon and the men are tracking down a possible location in Cuba where he stayed," Dominick added, joining them in the room.

Then Royce ran in. "We got it."

"What?" Giuseppe asked.

"We got a location. Star and his team are organizing a pre-operation and surveillance to see what we're up against. They say we need a lot of men on this. Dmitri is offering help, and of course, half of us to remain here and the others who can keep everything running smoothly while we go. Andriy said to come into the other room."

Giuseppe grabbed onto Andreas's arm and onto Dominick's shoulder. "We're going to get our woman back. Emanuel and his helpers must die. We can't leave anyone alive."

"I don't plan to leave anyone alive," Andreas stated firmly, and they hurried into the other room.

* * * *

Giada didn't feel grateful that Emanuel hadn't drugged her today. He wanted her walking on her own and reciprocating his touches and caresses. She wouldn't, though. She didn't think that would stop him from taking what he wanted from her. He was sick, twisted in the head, and he'd tricked her men, made them think that he'd raped her, was forcing himself between her legs, and he hadn't—not yet. But she wasn't stupid. He would rape her. To him it would mean the ultimate revenge against Dominick, specifically, for killing his brother but also against Andreas, Giuseppe, and the other families they were close to.

She shivered from his touch, forced to stand naked in front of him as he evaluated her body, complimented it, and then dressed her how he wanted. Tonight he put her in a blue see-through blouse with no bra and a light flared skirt in white, no panties. She wore no shoes, and her hair hung wildly around her shoulders because of the humidity of the island.

He brought a glass of wine to her lips. "To one of many romantic nights, Giada."

He pressed the glass to her mouth. She sealed her lips and refused to drink it. He gripped her jaw tight, forcing her to open her mouth. She struggled slightly, but she didn't want to show him she had strength. If she waited a little longer, maybe the aftereffects of the drugs would be worn off, and she could make a move. At this point, after the man had touched her so many times, whispered what he was going to do to her, and made her stay in his arms in his bed every night, she wanted to kill him. She just didn't know how or if she were physically capable of taking another person's life.

She swallowed the burning liquid, and he squinted at her. "You need discipline."

"Go to hell," she said.

The backhand to her mouth shocked her. The force was so great that she started to fall back in her chair when he gripped her by her hair to pull her forward. She shoved at his hands, and he struck her again then again. Her lips were bleeding, and her cheek throbbed in pain. He grabbed her neck and squeezed. Her chest was pressed against the table and her palm flat down on it. She felt the tips touch the large steak knife.

"I could end your life in a snap," he threatened her.

"Do it," she said, filled with fire and anger.

He chuckled and minimized her threat, and then the lights flashed. He looked around them, and she screamed out as she lifted the knife upward and slammed it down on his hand. He roared in anger, and she jumped up, felt weak and dizzy, but she didn't care. He grabbed at her top, ripping the sleeve, and she slammed his arm down and away from her. He shot a right hook at her, hitting her in the shoulder. She countered with an elbow. Then she grabbed the knife in his hand and yanked it out fast.

He roared again and went toward her as the lights went out completely, and she screamed, slammed the knife into his chest, and then turned to run. She heard him yelling in pain and then coming after her, despite her stabbing him. She was shaking, and her legs hardly worked as she tumbled down the stars and hit her forehead against the corner of the wooden railing.

"Get over here, bitch. What did you do?"

One of the guards grabbed her by her hair and yanked her up. She swung back at him, and he hit her with the butt of his gun. She was on the floor trying to fight him off, and she scrambled up his leg, throwing him off balance. He fell forward, and she gripped his gun, rolled to the right in one of her martial arts moves, and shot him three times.

Gunfire erupted all around the place, inside, outside, and she could see shadows through the windows. Men in black shooting at the guards, at Emanuel's men. She slowly started to head toward the side door when she heard the roar, turned, and Emanuel was there, lunging toward her with the knife in hand. She side-kicked, and he slashed her side. She screamed, and then the sounds of gunfire got closer, and men infiltrated the room she was in as she screamed and his body jerked as bullets hit him. Strong hands reached for her.

"Giada. It's Hadeon, Dmitri's guard," Hadeon said to her, and she cried out.

"Oh God."

"Got her."

"Where?" She could hear Andreas's voice through the receiver.

Then more men came through the doorway.

"Giada," Andreas yelled to her.

Then more shots were fired toward them, and Andreas, Hadeon, and the others fired back.

"We need to move," Hadeon said.

"What about Emanuel?" Andreas asked in anger.

"Your woman took care of him already."

As they headed out of the house and across the way, her legs felt weak, the adrenaline long gone. Andreas lifted her against his chest as they hurried into the jungle and then along the ocean shoreline. It seemed like forever until they got to a series of boats. More men were there.

"Our window of opportunity is closing in fast. Let's go," she heard a man with a thick Russian accent say, and then others spoke in another language.

They got onto the boat, and she held on to Andreas tight and couldn't stop shaking.

"Here, cover her up in this," one of the men said.

She felt the blanket go over her, and then the boats begin to move.

"It's over, Giada. It's all over." Andreas kissed her forehead, held her tight, and rocked her in his arms.

Epilogue

"How is she holding up? Is the therapy working?" Fedarro asked Andreas.

Andreas looked toward the table where Giada sat next to Giuseppe, holding on to his arm and listening to her friends talking.

"It's going to take time. She still can't sleep at night and wakes up jerking away from whichever one of us is holding her because she thinks it's Emanuel."

"Fuck that has to be tough. I'm sure with time it will pass. Who knows what he did to her. Plus, she was drugged, too."

"She said he didn't rape her. That's a positive. But he did touch her. He kept her drugged up in his bed, and he held her at night, made her lie there naked." Andreas ran his hands through his hair and then downed the rest of his drink.

Fedarro placed his hand on his shoulder. "It's over, Andreas. She fought hard when she needed to, and she stabbed that fucking dick. She shot another guy. She fought to get away from them and to get back to you, Dominick, and Giuseppe. Just love her, and everything else will work itself out."

Andreas exhaled and then nodded. "What are we going to do about Miami?"

"He's probably going to stay clear of any of us. He won't show his face because he knows his life is over. Sure we all wish he hadn't escaped, but he did, and if he comes anywhere near Giada, near any of our women or any of us, he's as good as dead. Plus, we have feelers out there looking for him, too."

"We aren't going to be taking any chances, Fedarro. Times are changing. The respect isn't there like it used to be."

"I agree," Fedarro said.

Then Andreas saw Dominick. He didn't look happy at all. He appeared angry and had been having a difficult time getting over Giada's abduction and how she'd been treated. He felt responsible.

"Dominick will come around, too. He needs to work this out his way. Giada's a strong woman, and she'll help him. She'll help all of you while you're helping her heal," Fedarro told him.

"I hope so, or else it's going to cause a wedge between them and between him, Giuseppe, and me. I try not to think of those videos and what Emanuel did to her and what she told us. I know she didn't share everything. I get that. Dominick needs more time to get past what happened and not blame himself."

"He will, Andreas. Just keep on him. Make sure he knows it wasn't his fault and to take this time to love Giada and be grateful she's alive and with the three of you. Remember, Mateus and I know how you feel. We could have lost Gisella."

Andreas nodded and looked back at the table where Giuseppe and Giada sat. It appeared that she wanted to get up.

* * * *

Giada sat between Giuseppe and Andreas on the ride back to the penthouse. Brew was in the passenger seat, and Train was driving. Behind them were Royce and Logic and another two vehicles of men. She held on to Andreas's hand and leaned against his side. Giuseppe kept a hand on her thigh, and she inhaled their scents, the familiar cologne, the feel of their masculinity and sizes. She looked down at her arm, still bandaged from the knife wound, but it was healing nicely. She closed her eyes and willed the uneasy feeling from her gut. She was safe now. As long as she was with one of her men and the security guys, she was safe. Emanuel was dead.

When the SUV stopped and parked in the underground parking garage, she felt anxious. It was a process she needed to work through. Lots of things frightened her, put her on edge, or made her feel antsy. Giuseppe offered his hand, and she took it but then waited for Andreas and took his hand, too. He slipped his arm around her back, and they walked with her together. Dominick was behind them. When they got into the elevator, she gripped their hands and waited until they got to the penthouse.

"Good night," Brew said to her.

She said good night to him and then the others. So did her men.

"Want something to drink?" Andreas asked her.

She shook her head. Dominick walked toward the windows and looked out with his hands on his hips. She could tell that Giuseppe and Andreas had noticed his demeanor. He had been keeping his distance. He seemed angry, and she knew he was trying to deal with everything that had happened, just like she had been. She needed them close to her, inside of her, and loving her.

She walked over to Dominick and slid under his arm. He immediately pulled her close, and she snuggled against him. His hand slid along her hip to her rear and back up again. She looked up at him. His chin tilted up, his eyes straight ahead. He felt tense, and his heart was racing. She heard it.

"Dominick, can you help me?" she asked him.

He looked down, squinting at her. "What do you need, baby?" He stared down into her eyes.

"You," she said to him, took his hand, and led him through the living room and to the bedroom. She glanced at Andreas and Giuseppe, who stood still, looking unsure. "Andreas and Giuseppe, I need you, too."

Dominick placed his hands on her hips and held her gaze as she began to unbutton his dress shirt. She slid her hands inside and inhaled his cologne.

"Your arm, baby."

"Is fine. You'll be careful. I know you'll take care of me."

He looked away, and she knew then for sure that he blamed himself for what had happened to her. She needed to fix this. She needed all of him. "I love you, Dominick. Don't you still love me?" She pressed his shirt away from his body.

"What? Of course I love you, Giada. More than anything, I do."

"Then stop blaming yourself for what happened to me. It was him, not you or your brothers or your cousin. There were a lot of factors. I shouldn't have gone to that door alone. I should have followed my gut about Uncle Les. I should have accepted more of your control without resistance. There are lots of things we all could have changed, and maybe what happened wouldn't have, but we can't do that. We can't live with regrets, with blaming ourselves. We're together, Dominick. You, me, Andreas, and Giuseppe. We're a family. You're all I have left in this world. You're all I'll ever need. Please, Dominick, I need you, each of you, to help me heal. To help me forget his touch, his words, his control, please, Dominick I—"

He pressed his lips to hers, kissing her deeply. His brothers and his cousin joined in undressing her, and when Dominick pulled from her lips, he stepped from his pants as Andreas unzipped her dress. They were naked in no time, and Dominick lifted her and placed her gently onto the bed. He looked at her body from above. He stroked her nipple then along her ribs. She shivered and shook.

"Love me."

"Always.' He lowered down between her legs and licked her pussy.

Andreas and Giuseppe climbed onto the bed and joined him. They kissed her skin from wrists to shoulders and from nipples and breasts to her belly. They each took turns licking and sucking her cream from her cunt then positioning her to their liking. She absorbed it all—their hands, not his; their mouths, not his; their loving touch that healed her inch by inch and kiss by kiss.

As she climbed onto Dominick, she slid her wet pussy right over his cock and exhaled. "I missed you so," she whispered.

He cupped her breasts. "Not as much as I missed you."

She smiled, lowered, and kissed his mouth. She started with the corners then the center and along his chin and neck then back up to his lips just as Andreas slid a finger of lube to her anus. Giuseppe caressed her hair, and she turned to look at him. He was a god, with his tan complexion and his large hand fisting his cock and stroking it.

"Can you?" he asked.

"I want to," she said and lowered her mouth to his cock and licked the tip before pulling him into her mouth. Her body adjusted to the familiar feel of her men taking from her body, claiming her again. She felt the tightness in her core, and then Andreas pulled out his fingers and replaced them with his cock. He slid into her ass, and they all exhaled in relief and pleasure. Very slowly, almost in a tortuous manner, her men stroked their cocks into her, made love to her, empowered their bond with every stroke.

"Heaven. Inside of you is heaven," Dominick said.

Then they started to move faster, deeper.

"I'm there, baby." Giuseppe came in her mouth.

She licked him clean, and he kissed her cheeks and her mouth after he pulled out and slid from the bed. Andreas came next and then her, along with Dominick. They rolled her to the side, cleaned her up, and cared for her. She clung to Dominick and kissed his chest as Andreas kissed her spine, her ass, and then her shoulders and Giuseppe kissed her calves and ran a hand up her thigh and calf over and over again as he lay at the bottom of the bed.

She smiled and closed her eyes. This was happiness, success, and completion. She had her three men to cherish and love, men who would protect her, care for her, and love her every day. The money, the power, the fancy cars, and high-priced items didn't mean anything at all. The love they shared did. The power of their bond did. That was what life was all about. She was the richest woman alive.

THE END

WWW.DIXIELYNNDWYER.COM

Siren Publishing, Inc.
www.SirenPublishing.com

Lightning Source UK Ltd.
Milton Keynes UK
UKHW02f2144211117
313124UK00013B/794/P

9 781640 108295